C. S. F

Cecil Scott Forester, an Englishman, was born in Cairo in 1899, the son of a British army officer. He was educated in London, and after World War I service in the infantry, he decided to be a poet. This was a short-lived pursuit and he soon turned to biography and fiction.

He then wrote many best-selling novels—*African Queen* and *The General* among them—before he wrote the first of his Hornblower stories. That first book, in 1937, was *Beat to Quarters*, chronologically the fifth volume in the career of the inimitable Hornblower.

In April of 1966, while writing *Hornblower During the Crisis*, C. S. Forester died. Today, the popularity of his writing still continues to grow, and the names of both Forester and Hornblower have become synonymous with the greatest names in naval literature.

By the same Author:

THE HORNBLOWER SERIES

THE MAN
in the
YELLOW RAFT
by
C.S. FORESTER

PINNACLE BOOKS · NEW YORK CITY

THE MAN IN THE YELLOW RAFT

Copyright © 1942, 1943, 1945, © 1969 by Dorothy E. Forester

Copyright © 1961, 1962 by C. S. Forester

A Pinnacle Books edition, published by special arrangement with Little, Brown and Company.

ISBN: 0-523-00839-2

First printing, April 1976

Cover illustration by Chuck McVicker

Printed in the United States of America

PINNACLE BOOKS, INC.
275 Madison Avenue
New York, N. Y. 10016

THE MAN IN THE YELLOW RAFT

The Man in the Yellow Raft

In United States destroyer *Boon* the babies had grown into adolescents overnight apparently, and all the troubles associated with adolescence were making their appearance. Until now the troubles had been those of infancy, arising mostly out of simple ignorance or innocence; but after the victory that *Boon* had gained there was a very noticeable change. *Boon* had sailed from Mare Island with a ship's company of whom more than one third had been recruits, men of the best quality, all volunteers who had joined the Navy before Pearl Harbor. Boot camp had changed them very little; they had been law-abiding in intention, at least, and so interested in their new life that initiating them in their duties had been like playing nursery games with toddlers—toddlers armed with weapons their grandfathers had never dreamed of. Thanks to those weapons, they had ambushed and destroyed a Japanese cruiser, gaining a victory that had echoed round the world, and with that victory, and after three months at sea, the toddlers had grown up into teen-agers.

Now they knew everything that was worth knowing; and no one could show them anything. The attention paid to rules and conventions by their seniors was tiresome; it also marked those seniors down as conservative old men sinking into decrepitude. The community in which the recruits found themselves appeared to them to be both inelastic and old-fashioned; they were sure that from their fresh point of view they could visualise a better system. Moreover, they knew so much more about the rules and conventions now, that those among them who were merely irked in their way of life by the restrictions could think of ways of circumventing them. The infants had been pleased and proud to be playing in a group game; the teen-agers resented, consciously or unconsciously, the merging of their precious individualities into a single entity.

The consequence was—as other communities have found—the development of a wave of crime. The *Boon*, when she resumed her course and headed southwestward again across the Pacific, was engulfed in crime. The Japanese cruiser lay a thousand fathoms deep behind her, a rived wreck on the dark floor of the ocean, while the men who had destroyed her celebrated their victory by perfectly shocking behaviour. One heavenly still night, as the *Boon* coursed onward over the dark swell, George Brown, the executive officer, awoke in his cabin to hear a noise that should never be heard in a ship of war; an instantly recognisable noise like no other. He left his bunk and went below; his microscopic familiarity with every corner of the ship directed his steps straight to the source of the noise. As he stepped across a high coaming he heard it once more; the unmistakable sound of a pair of dice rattling over a steel deck and bouncing back from a steel bulkhead.

2

"Snake eyes!" said one of the squatting group, and it was certainly the most unlucky throw of the evening, for that was when they looked up to find the executive officer standing over them.

"Whose money is this?" asked that officer, but no one would admit ownership, not even when he went on: "Nobody's? If it's unclaimed I shall have to take charge of it for the Ship's Welfare Fund."

They eyed him silently as he picked it up; there was a five-dollar bill, as well as several ones and some quarters and dimes. "Thirteen dollars and twenty cents," said the executive officer. "You men can turn in now."

The United States Navy was not concerned with morals, viewed simply as morals, even though there were Congressmen who wished otherwise. The Navy was a fighting body, with victory as its aim. Victory or defeat, as well as life or death, depended on the last ounce of effort, the highest pitch of efficiency; and the Navy had convinced itself that craps on board could cut down the effort and reduce the efficiency of the men. Gambling led to bitterness, to feuds; it led to a possible relaxation of discipline between debtors and creditors, to possible lapses from duty.

Brown looked along the line of criminals and remembered something else. "You, Carducci. You're due to come up to captain's mast this morning. Aren't you?"

"Yes, sir."

"Sleeping on watch."

"Yes, sir."

"This may help to explain it."

It did nothing to explain it in the mind of Fireman

2nd Class Pietro Carducci. His job was standing duty at the evaporator, watching the water level, and he could see no connection between a harmless crap game at midnight and nodding off in the four to eight. The water level in the evaporator had remained constant, of course, and there had been no harm done, even though he would freely admit, from his own knowledge, that the gravest damage to the evaporator might have ensued had the level fallen. To Fireman Carducci the linking of the two charges was only one more example of the way in which the Navy was ready to hang a dog to which it had already given a bad name.

At captain's mast he was consoled to some extent by the misfortunes of his friend Fireman 2nd Class Clover, found guilty of a quite different crime. Clover had not turned off the tap of the shower bath, having stepped out of it to soap himself after going under to get wet. A regulation laid it down that the tap should not be left running during those thirty seconds, and Clover readily admitted that he had not observed the regulation.

"And yet you knew the order?" asked the captain. "Wet down. Turn off. Soap down. Turn on. Rinse down. Turn off."

"Yes, sir."

There were several listeners who could not see any connection between fighting the Japs and the meaningless ritual the captain had just recited.

"You wasted two gallons of fresh water," said the captain, eyeing the boy before him, whose bewilderment hid behind a sullen mask.

Two hundred men could waste four hundred gallons of fresh water a day; fifty tons in a month, and that would mean the consumption of half a ton of fuel. Captain Angell, looking over the head of the man before him, could picture in his mind's eye *Boon*, with nearly empty bunkers, crawling perforce at slowest economical speed across the Pacific, exposed at every moment to submarine attack.

He met the boy's eyes again; it was no use making a little speech along these lines. They had just sunk a Japanese cruiser with apparently the greatest of ease, and nothing at the moment could convince these lads of the importance of two gallons of fresh water.

"Five hours' extra duty," said the captain. It was a poor way, he knew, of trying to impress the importance of water economy on Clover's mind, but it was the only way possible at present.

The captain went on to lecture Seaman 2nd Class Helder on the enormity of being late relieving watch: and the last criminal on the list was Seaman 2nd Class Kortland. The captain took special note of this man. An intelligent-looking man of sensitive expression; as a high-school graduate he was a man of some education. Of course he was a man only by courtesy of the Navy, seeing that he was still only eighteen. And his crime was something a little out of the ordinary; his battle station was in the lower handling room of the No. 1 five-inch gun, and he had apparently formed the habit of settling down there, among the live shells, for an hour or two of peace and quiet after the ship secured from morning general quarters. The captain felt a certain sympathy for him, but no one could possibly be allowed to remain unsupervised

5

down among the ammunition, apart from all the other considerations.

"Five hours' extra duty," said the captain.

"Mast cases dismissed," said the executive officer.

"You know," announced the executive officer in the wardroom later, "the British have the right idea with their rum ration."

"I know plenty who'd agree with you," said Lieutenant Klein.

"What makes you say it at this moment, George?" asked the captain, taking a first sip at his coffee. "What's the peculiar virtue of the rum ration today?"

"There's no virtue in the issue of a rum ration," said the executive officer.

"Shame!" interjected Klein.

"But there's a lot of virtue in taking it away. What can we do to a man out here when he bucks the regulations? Extra duty? You reach a limit with that in no time—all the men have pretty well all they can do already, and you've got to be careful with their health. Restriction? They've given up hope of ever seeing port again, and restriction doesn't mean a thing. Loss of pay? Pay doesn't mean anything out here either, especially now that we've dealt with the crap games."

"Are you telling *us*, sir?" asked Lieutenant Borglum.

"So there's no way of getting at the man who's lazy or careless, or who thinks he knows it all already. But leading this sort of life you come to look forward to it from day to day, just as a break in the monotony, perhaps. Take it away, and you've really done something. Next time he'll be more careful. I'm all for a

6

rum ration, in wartime conditions anyway," the executive officer finished.

"Maybe you have something there," agreed Borglum.

"Maybe Josephus Daniels is turning in his grave," said Klein. "Are you going to bring flogging back too, sir?"

"It's just about as likely," admitted the executive officer.

Two days later—two days more of monotonous steaming across the featureless Pacific—Klein made a handsome admission.

"I've come round to your way of thinking, sir," he said. "That fellow Kortland. The man who used to hide away in the lower handling room. You know about the new offence, of course?"

"I've just published the deck court you held," said the executive officer.

"You have? How did the captain feel about the sentence?"

"He remitted part of it. Now it stands at fifteen days' restriction."

"Fifteen or twenty—what's the difference? It's just what you were saying. For the next fifteen days he'll watch his pals pouring ashore to enjoy themselves while he has to stay on board. Oh, yes, and he'll lose about twenty dollars in pay. A lot he cares."

"And insubordination is a serious charge. I know he sassed the chief boatswain's mate, but what did he say?"

"I expect Trautmann had been riding him some. You know Kortland's the compartment cleaner and scullery maid for the c.p.o.'s quarters?"

"Yes. Nice job. Doesn't stand watches."

"He hadn't cleaned up the soap dishes in the head, and Trautmann checked him for it."

"Well?"

"So he flared out. He said, 'I'm not a servant. I'll do it when I'm good and ready'."

"He must be just a plain fool."

"I'm not so sure. He lost his temper. It's not so long since he had a mother running round after him cleaning the soap dishes."

"Yes. But insubordination—"

There was no need to finish the sentence. With the safety of the ship, with victory or defeat depending on instant obedience, a state of mind must never be allowed to exist wherein it was possible to argue back or hesitate to obey. To the two officers this was self-evident, a part of life. It was not so evident to a recent high-school boy, however.

"Oh, well," said the executive officer, "tempers are short just now. But we're making contact with the task force tomorrow. That'll be a break in the monotony and may do everyone good. Maybe Kortland will learn sense."

Seaman 2nd Class Charles Kortland was not a fool, but a mixed-up boy still, a nice-looking boy, incidentally; that fact had a bearing on the circumstances leading up to his present state of mind. On his graduation from high school the previous summer he had persuaded a doting mother to allow him to anticipate the draft and enlist in the Navy. Eight months in the service had been just enough to muddle his thinking without making a man of him. As a handsome only child he had never known anything except his own

8

way; as an only child he had come to enjoy solitude; and his doting mother had encouraged him in his belief that there was no one in the world quite so important or quite so worthy of every attention as Charles Kortland. And the Navy never allowed him his own way; it offered almost no chance of enjoying solitude; and it did not share—it laughed at—his estimate of his own importance.

His present job, as compartment cleaner to the chief petty officers' quarters, was one many on board would have coveted; it was one of those given in rotation, in fact, for that reason. But Kortland resented having to clean up after other people; he had a poor opinion of chief petty officers, which did not make it any easier, and helped to explain the outburst which had brought him a deck court-martial. The desire for extra sleep had not been the cause of his stolen hours in the lower handling room; he had only wanted to get away by himself—the hardest thing in the world in a wartime destroyer. So now he was standing and chipping paint along with a group of other hardened criminals, completing the last hour of the sentence which had condemned him to this work before the deck court-martial. His fingers were sore by the time he was released.

"Sail ho!" yelled a lookout on the flying bridge.

"Where away?"

"Dead ahead."

Right ahead; *Boon* had made visual contact at last with other ships of the United States Navy, after eleven days of complete solitude. The effect was felt in every part of the ship, and all to the good, as the executive officer had predicted. There were other ships

9

to look at now, instead of an empty horizon, and disparaging comparisons to be made between them and the *Boon*. There was a tanker to refuel from, calling for considerable activity on the part of the first lieutenant and Chief Boatswain's Mate Trautmann and their party. There were new faces to be seen along the tanker's rail, and old jests to be refurbished and hurled back and forth across the foaming water that divided the two ships while the fuelling proceeded.

There was no mail—that was too much to hope for—but there was fresh bread, enough for two meals, to be hauled on board over the "pony express"; there was ice cream, enough for a couple of dips per man, to follow. And there was a batch of new movies; from the deck of the tanker came the most stimulating comments about the new musical featuring Alice Faye, which at that moment was travelling over to *Boon* along the high line. Every eye that could be spared from duty watched the bundle with passionate anxiety until it arrived safely.

The whole world was in a turmoil, and the destiny of mankind hung in the balance. The men who lined those rails knew—if they stopped to think about it— that their lives were in imminent deadly peril, that mutilation or death might be their portion at any moment. Yet all these issues were obscured at this moment by the prospect of fresh bread, ice cream and the shadow of Miss Alice Faye upon a screen.

"Movies tonight, man!" said Seaman 2nd Class Henderson ecstatically to Seaman 2nd Class Kortland.

"Yeah," agreed Kortland. He at least was not going

10

to be so undignified as to display all the enthusiasm he actually felt.

An announcement over the ship's loudspeaker added to the pleasure and excitement he was concealing. "Now hear this. Now hear this. Now that the ship has joined the task force the ship will not go to general quarters at sunset until further notice. The ship will not go to general quarters . . ."

Kortland did not bother to listen to the repetition. His quick mind was foreseeing new possibilities. The c.p.o.'s ate their dinner early. If there were no general quarters he could get through his scullery maid's duties early and could be down in the mess hall well before anyone else in the ship; he could pick himself a seat, settle himself down at leisure and view the show from a position of advantage, in comparative comfort, and without an undignified preliminary scramble.

He liked movies and tonight he would be able to enjoy them in the leisurely and privileged way that was really his due. That was how it came about that the executive officer, passing through the mess hall before the show was ready to start, grinned at the sight of the young seaman stalking down alone from the other end with an exaggerated air of owning the place, and seating himself before the centre of the screen. The exec picked him out among the crowd after the movie was over, too; the expression on his face showed how much he had enjoyed his evening.

The *Boon* was still a stepchild among destroyers; the task force to which she was attached included not one ship of her division. She was a newcomer, too, and this helped to explain why she was given the odd jobs to do, and why she was stationed on the wing

11

of the destroyer screen that combed the sea above and below the surface, in advance of the main body, as the task force steamed steadily northward into dangerous waters. A battle had been fought in the Coral Sea; there had been losses on both sides as they groped for each other, each trying to guess at the other's objectives. The wildest stories had been told, and some of them had even proved true. While naval staffs tried to evaluate results, and while a puzzled world was coming slowly to the conclusion that the newest Japanese advance had been beaten back, this little task force was moving in to maintain an appearance of strength.

The Japanese would strike again; no one could doubt it. But the American naval staffs had already shrewdly guessed that the blow would be delivered elsewhere, against Midway, the Aleutians, against Pearl Harbor itself. There was every reason to convey the impression that the United States Navy was massing to defend New Guinea and Australia again, leaving Midway unguarded. This was the business of the little task force. Seaman 2nd Class Charles Kortland, with all his personal problems, washing dishes in the chief petty officers' pantry, was playing his part in the preliminary moves of the decisive naval battle of the war.

The sun was shining bright that morning when *Boon* secured from general quarters and Kortland came up on deck from his battle station down in the lower handling room. The sky was blue, and the sea was bluer still, with a segment of gold extending to the horizon, above which hung the golden sun; and behind, the ships stretched their long parallel wakes dazzling white against the blue. A lovely morning, and tonight he was going to see Alice Faye in the musical. He entered the chief petty officers' pantry to encounter harsh reality.

"Do you see this?" asked Chief Boatswain's Mate Trautmann. He was pointing at the garbage can, too full for the lid to close properly, and beside it the bulging paper sack that held the excess. "I said, 'Do you see this?'" said Trautmann.

"Yes," Kortland blurted out, for not to answer would be an additional offence.

"It's stinking already and it will have to go on stinking. Any excuse?"

Not even Kortland's quick mind could think of one in that surprised moment. He had forgotten about the garbage last night in the excitement of going to the movies. Regulations were explicit that it should only be dumped after sunset so as to leave the least traces for a scouting enemy. He had intended to return and dump the garbage after the movies and had forgotten all about it. Now it would have to stay on board all day.

"Any excuse?" repeated Trautmann.

"No."

"You'll be at captain's mast this morning."

And when he came up before the captain he had to stand at attention and listen to a short lecture.

"This is the third time you've been in trouble," said the captain. "I can't understand why an intelligent fellow like you should behave in this way. This time it will be ten hours' extra duty."

Kortland had sense enough not to allow his feelings to appear. He could live through ten hours of paint chipping without noticing it, as long as he had the prospect of Alice Faye this evening. But before he could be dismissed the executive officer interposed.

"Excuse me, sir. Do you remember the British, sir? You—"

"Yes, I remember," said the captain. Half an hour ago the executive officer had pointed out to him that movies meant as much to Kortland as rum to a Britisher, and had indicated a course of action. The captain went on. "This extra duty will be served as lookout during the second dog watch for the next five days."

There was an astonished silence at this new departure.

"Would you mind repeating that, sir?" asked the ship's yeoman, who was noting the proceedings.

The captain had no objection. He repeated what he had said, clearly and distinctly, and again there was silence.

"Mast dismissed," said the executive officer.

Kortland was actually pale, tanned though he was, as he turned away. Some of the pallor was due to surprise and disappointment, but some of it was caused by rage. Not merely would he not get a front seat for Alice Faye but he would miss all but the end of the picture. His world fell away from him as he thought about it. When captain's mast was finished he saw the exec walking aft to inspect the after-gun mount, and he had the wild notion, momentarily, of appealing to him for his good offices in changing the order; but he knew enough about the Navy for the notion to be only momentary. And as he looked across at the exec, he had a moment of revelation. He remembered how

14

the first night before the movies started he had met the exec's eyes before choosing his seat. That man had eyes for everything. Kortland did not understand the reference to the captain; it might even be a code word. But that just showed he was the victim of a persecution directed with diabolical ingenuity. He felt friendless and betrayed. It was enough—nearly—to make a man weep, or to drive him to violence.

Kortland was man enough not to weep and sensible enough not to indulge in violence. Just before sunset each dog watch he climbed up to the flying bridge and took his assigned place on the starboard side to begin his dreary spell as lookout, staring out over the wide waste of blue water while the *Boon* and the rest of the task force steamed on northward, soaring slowly up the long, endless swells, and slithering down the farther slopes, the angle of meeting the swell varying irregularly with the irregular scheme of zigzagging. *Boon* was the right-hand ship of the screen, and he was the right-hand man of the ship; with misery contending with resentment in his heart he was guarding the right flank of the task force. He could hardly help but take his duties seriously, even though at the same time a dozen sonar apparatuses were probing the depths below him, and the ship's radar was scanning the horizon all round. Neither radar nor sonar could be implicitly trusted; they could not report smoke or wreckage. For that matter even after nightfall the human eye still had its uses. Even in a ship where they made silly jokes about borrowing from the British.

On the third night the sun was sinking in a clear sky over on his left hand; behind him, in fact, when he faced out to starboard and the zigzag took a westerly trend. It was dreary, monotonous work, unsuited to a thinking mind, decided Kortland as usual. A thousand hours of monotony and repetition for one hour of Alice Faye, and then to be tricked out of Alice Faye in the end. It was Alice Faye and not the Japanese who occupied his thoughts—he was like nearly every one of his shipmates in that respect.

Now the sun was hanging just above the horizon and giving perceptibly less light as it reddened. *Boon* climbed a swell, and as she hung on the summit Kortland, looking out to starboard, caught a momentary flash on the horizon. It had come and gone at once; it had been the faintest speck of light, as though a wet surface had for a second reflected the reddening sun behind him. He glued his eyes on the spot and waited. He might have been mistaken; it might have been merely a wave top. The seconds passed, lengthened into a minute. No; as the *Boon* hung on the next summit there it was—a wet surface catching the light. He wondered what he should do, and it should be noted that his resentment was not in evidence as he debated with himself. He was much more preoccupied with the fear of making a fool of himself. *Boon* climbed the next swell, and there it was again, this time briefer than ever if that were possible, and redder than before. Kortland took a deep breath.

"Sail ho!" he yelled down to the bridge.

Instant tension down below; the Navy endured ten thousand hours of monotony and repetition in preparation for an hour of battle.

"Where away?" from the officer of the deck.

"Broad on the starboard beam. An—an object, sir. I saw it catch the light, sir."

Every eye that could be spared was turned out to starboard. Only the briefest flash this time, and only Kortland, with his eyes trained in exactly the right direction, spotted it.

"There it is, sir!"

This second definite identification made up the mind of the officer of the deck.

"Captain to the bridge," he said to the man at the voice tube.

Kortland was fully committed now. It took only a moment for the captain to reach the bridge, and a moment more for the executive officer to follow him.

"Do you think he's seeing things?" asked the captain.

"Who is it up there? Oh, it's young Kortland," said the executive officer, and then, "I think we can trust him."

Half the sun was below the horizon, and darkness was increasing apace.

"Tell us what you saw again, Kortland," hailed the captain.

"I saw something catch the light, sir. It might be wreckage."

"Are you sure of the bearing?"

"Yes, sir." Kortland's pointed arm indicated it with a promise of exactitude.

The sun was gone now, as the captain wrestled with his problem. As soon as it was fully night the task force was to reverse course and steam south again; it would be awkward for a detached destroyer to resume her place in the screen in darkness. But still—

The captain reached his decision. "Keep your eye on the place, Kortland," he said before he went to the radio telephone. "Request permission to investigate an unidentified object to starboard, sir. . . . Aye, aye, sir. Thank you."

In the fading light *Boon* swung herself round until her jack staff was right in line with Kortland's pointed arm and then she headed forward with increased revolutions. Darker and darker it grew, and then another lookout took up the cry.

"I see it, sir! Dead ahead! A rubber life raft!" Now they could all see it.

"All engines stop."

Boon's speed slowly diminished.

"All engines back one third."

It was very nearly completely dark as *Boon* surged alongside; it was indeed a yellow rubber life raft whose wet side had reflected the sunset back to Kortland's eye, and lying in it was a U.S. Navy aviator; it was not until they had hoisted him on board that they could be sure he was alive. The battle of the Coral Sea had been fought ten long, long days ago. Kortland could look down upon the nearly lifeless thing swinging up on the line.

The following afternoon Kortland was mildly surprised to hear the ship's loudspeaker say his name. The call interrupted a furious train of thought; the films were to be returned tomorrow, and the whole ship's company, when consulted, had selected the Alice Faye musical as the movie to be repeated tonight. And he still had extra duty to perform, and he would miss Alice Faye for the second time.

18

"Seaman 2nd Class Kortland to report to the bridge immediately."

Waiting there was the pharmacist's mate 1st class who tried to watch over the health of the entire ship's company.

"You're going to see Lieutenant Evans, the naval aviator you spotted on the rubber life raft," said the pharmacist's mate. "He wants to thank you. This way."

He led the way to the captain's cabin, the one the captain never slept in at sea.

"Exec's given permission," explained the pharmacist's mate.

The bunk there held a young man, incredibly thin, with brilliant dark eyes glittering out of a face tanned almost black, patchily, because some of that face was much whiter where ten days' beard had been shaved off.

"It was you who saved my life," said the lieutenant. "I want to thank you."

"Yes, sir," said Kortland. It was an unhelpful thing to say at this moment.

"Another night in that boat and I'd have had it," went on the lieutenant. "And it wasn't easy for you— they've told me about it."

"It wasn't anything, sir," said Kortland. He had his dignity to consider, even though the pharmacist's mate constituted the entire audience.

"We can't go on arguing about it," said the lieutenant. "The exec's as pleased as hell about what you did. He gave permission for me to send for you so as to give me a chance to talk to you. I'm being transferred tomorrow. Now you tell me. What do you

19

want? I've only got to ask the exec and he'll give it to
you. What would you like?"

Alice Faye tonight. But on the other hand there
was that remark about borrowing from the British.
That rankled, although Kortland still had no idea
what it meant; yet there were other things that he
understood. He was perfectly aware, with acute telep-
athy, that the exec was ready and willing to excuse
him from the rest of his extra duty. And somewhere
in his subconscious there was a revolt against the in-
congruity of relating the saving of a life to an exhi-
bition of shadows on a screen. Even though Kortland
was growing up fast he was still a mixed-up teen-ager.
He opened his mouth to speak and shut it again just
in time—he had been about to say, "To hell with the
British," and that would have made just no sense to
the lieutenant nor to the pharmacist's mate.

"Well?" asked the lieutenant.

Kortland had to prove that the British were wrong,
that the exec was wrong, and that he himself was a
man who did not care about movies in the least.

"I don't want anything," said Kortland. "I don't
want anything at all."

It was three seconds later before he remembered
what else he should have said, and he added it. "Sir."

Triumph of the *Boon*

The Navy lieutenant stepped down from the DC-3—what the Navy called an R4D—in a rainstorm which in one minute wetted every stitch of clothing he was wearing. It roared down upon him with a violence that might have been stupefying, except that the other factors that instantly assailed his senses were so violent also that he could not help taking note of them.

First there was the stink which filled his nostrils. Basically it was the stink of all low-lying tropical land, except that in Guadalcanal it asserted itself with unequalled intensity. Moreover it was backed up by a host of other stinks, most of them based on corruption but some based on the stale fumes of high explosives.

The lieutenant took note of the stench, for he could do nothing else, but immediately afterward he received his next impression, which was one of mud. Mud everywhere; the airstrip on which he trod was a "Marsden Mat" made of perforated metal strips, but the mud seeped up through the perforations so that foothold was precarious, and to walk upon the metal conveyed the feeling that below it lay a bottomless quagmire, as was indeed the case.

The first people the lieutenant saw in Guadalcanal

21

seemed to be adding to the mud, for they were filling a shell crater from a dump truck. The lieutenant understood, when he saw what they were doing, why the DC-3 had bounced along the airstrip like a boat at sea when making its landing. And he had hardly taken more than a few steps before a roar and a muffled crash, blending with and accentuating the roar of the rain, heralded the appearance of a mud volcano, as a five-inch shell pitched on to the far end of the strip and flung up a huge fountain of mud and metal.

"Come along to the general," said someone to the lieutenant.

That was the next impression; one of pressure. And like the stink, that impression was backed up by minor ingredients. There was strain, and there were fatigue and the feeling of insufficient materials with which to undertake all the tasks that demanded attention. Yet one ingredient was missing—and its absence was the next and perhaps the most striking impression of all. There was no hint of despair. Maybe—probably largely—this was due to the presence of the general to whose command post the lieutenant was escorted.

"Lieutenant Borglum reporting from the *Boon,* sir," said the lieutenant, and even while he spoke he was conscious of encountering a solid personality—nothing flashy, nothing theatrical, but completely fearless in every sense.

"Glad to see you, lieutenant," said the general. Borglum noticed that the general was newly shaven, in contrast with the fuzzy-cheeked individuals he had met so far, and then he observed scratches on the general's cheeks—it was a dull razor blade which had done that job.

The general spoke again after five seconds spent in measuring up the young man in front of him. "I might even say I'm mighty glad to see you, lieutenant. I could have had half a drum of gasoline instead, if you want proof of what I say."

"Yes, sir."

"Gasoline," said the general. "Gasoline here in these devil-haunted islands. If we have it, we win. If we don't have it, Uncle Sam will receive a setback that he'll find expensive. You can't say that a thousand gallons here is worth a million Stateside. Nor ten million. The value is beyond all ordinary figures."

"Yes, sir."

"Mahan pointed out to Annapolis that sea power brings with it command of the sea, and command of the sea means freedom to use the sea and the ability to deny its use to the enemy."

"Yes, sir."

"There weren't any threats from aeroplanes in Mahan's time, but the principle remains the same."

"Yes, sir."

"Around this island, aeroplanes are one element of sea power. If we have 'em and can put 'em in the air, we control the waters all round, and we win. If we don't have 'em, or we can't put 'em in the air, we don't."

"Of course, sir," Borglum offered.

"The United States Navy and the Japanese Navy are at full stretch at this point. Command of the air is the deciding factor."

"Yes, sir."

"Now we come to the point, lieutenant. Seventy-two hours from now, give or take an hour or two, and I shall be unable to put a fighter plane in the air. No gasoline."

"Good God!"

"It's as simple as that. It's as serious as that, lieutenant."

"I didn't realise it, sir."

"You know it now. That's why I want the *Boon* to bring me gasoline."

"Yes, sir. I understand."

"The R4D's just can't bring enough in. AKA's are too slow and vulnerable. It's up to the *Boon*."

"Yes, sir."

There was a shriek of a siren and the crash of high explosives at this moment. The general cocked his ear skyward to gauge the extent of the danger.

"I don't think we need take action, lieutenant. Let's get down to brass tacks." He reached for a map. "Here's Ringdove Shoal."

The technical details of exactly where the destroyer *Boon* should drop her cargo of gasoline were settled in five minutes' discussion.

"It's not enough just to drop the drums overboard," said the general. "They've got to reach shore. *Boon*'ll have to wash them on the beach."

"Naturally, sir."

"Drop 'em over on the westward run. Do I have to remind you to give 'em plenty of buoyancy?"

"No, sir."

"You won't be able to make more than two or

24

three knots while you're doing it. Then you turn and come back at twenty—twenty-five, maybe. Shallow water, a narrow channel between the shore and the shoals. You'll kick up something like a tidal wave, and that'll bring the drums in to where we can get 'em."

"Yes, sir."

"That's settled then." The general studied the young man closely again. "I'm going to tell you something else, lieutenant. There's no harm in your knowing it, and there's no harm in everyone in your ship knowing it. And your captain has to know it."

"Yes, sir." Borglum could not guess what piece of information could possibly be such public property in wartime.

"This is a priority mission. Nothing else is of any importance. *Nothing*, lieutenant. *Boon* is not to be diverted from this primary objective for any reason at all. She has to deliver two hundred drums of high octane gasoline. You understand?"

"Yes, sir."

"It's been a pleasure to make your acquaintance, lieutenant."

The dismissal was polite and abrupt in curious combination, leaving Borglum free for the rest of the day to taste all the experiences Guadalcanal had to offer—the heat and the mosquitoes as well as the mud and the rain and the stink; the miserable scenery of the marshy flats squeezed in between the mountains and the sea, for Guadalcanal, while being at that moment the most important island in the whole Pacific, owed that importance to the mere five per cent of its area that was comparatively level.

At nightfall Borglum went back on board the R4D. The importance of his mission was accentuated in his mind by the sight of the wounded who lay there. The thought of that gave intensity to his report to Captain Angell when the R4D brought him back to Espiritu Santo.

This was at two o'clock in the morning; ten minutes after the jeep had deposited him near the anchorage, Borglum had wakened the executive officer, and ten minutes after that the two of them had wakened Captain Angell; the best proof of the urgency Borglum displayed lay in the fact that Brown, the executive officer, should take the responsibility of breaking into his captain's rest.

They sat in the stifling blacked-out cabin, the two senior officers listening while Borglum poured out his account of the interview with the general.

Angell referred again to the orders from Southwest Pacific that had come in that evening, and he looked again at the chart spread on the table. Brown tapped with his pencil at one point of the chart.

"You see that, sir?"

"'Strong tide rips occasionally.' Yes, I've noticed it."

Brown took the dividers and measured the line he had ruled on the other chart.

"Twenty-four hours at twenty knots, sir," he announced. "That will bring us to here, the southeast tip of the island."

"That's where we want to be at sunset. Not before," said Angell. "Let's say twenty miles east of the point.

Then we can go up outside Nura in the dark and turn west for the run into the channel."

"Yes, sir," agreed Brown, dividers at work again. "That brings us out at daylight back off the point again. Two hours' margin, let's say, sir."

"Good enough."

Angell had taken paper and pencil and appeared to be idly sketching. The outline of a destroyer's deck took shape on the paper. Within the outline he marked in the plan of the destroyer's upper works.

"This is the way it'll have to be done," he said. "We'll want runways all along here on both sides. It had better be four-by-fours—those drums weigh nearly five hundred pounds each. And we'll want guards on each quarter to shoot 'em clear. Don't want 'em in the props. You'll have to see about that tonight, Mr. Borglum."

"Aye aye, sir."

"Call the carpenter and go ashore with him. You can use the jeep. You'll have to wake 'em up there and get 'em going, so as to have the stuff ready for us by daylight. We're going to have a busy day."

It was the end of a momentary glimpse of paradise for all hands in the *Boon*. Paradise it had been, for two whole days—only one for Lieutenant Borglum. With an anchor at the bow *Boon*'s stern had actually been held ashore by a cable to a palm tree. Overside there had been the best swimming in the world and the best fishing too, for that matter.

Of course it was too good to last. Every man told himself that, when the end came an hour before daylight and he was roused to a day of violent activity.

"We might have known," said Seaman Second Class Kortland to Seaman Second Class Helder.

"Get going," said Chief Bosun's Mate Trautmann.

"We ought to find room for two hundred and eight drums," said Angell to Brown.

"Four hundred and ten pounds each," said Brown, and plunged into a calculation. "Thirty-eight tons, sir, and a good bit of it aft. That'll give the screws a better bite. We'll have to remember that, sir. We'll be making more speed over the ground than the turns'll indicate."

"Just one more thing to remember when the time comes," agreed Angell.

Two hundred and eight drums of gasoline, each weighing one fifth of a ton, had to be hoisted aboard the *Boon* by the ship's davits and then manhandled into position along each side of the ship, under a sweltering sun that the need for violent activity had changed since yesterday from a beneficent heavenly body to a malignant enemy. But before those drums could be hoisted on board each one needed special treatment. From each there had to be extracted four gallons of gasoline to provide the positive buoyancy that the general had demanded.

Not only that; when a drum of gasoline was destined to be thrown into the sea and cast up on shore by the surf, no reliance could be placed on the plug which sealed it. Every plug after being screwed home had to be covered with hot tar, and every seal coaxed to adhere to the inhospitable surface.

All along the deck of the *Boon*, from forward aft on both sides, the runways of four-by-fours had to be fixed in position. On them would rest thirty-eight tons of cargo, not on a stable base on shore, but on the deck of a ship rolling wildly in a seaway— rolling the more wildly with this additional weight above the waterline.

Naturally the deck had a camber; it was domed upward both to support the weight of seas bursting aboard and to hasten their departure after bursting. Now that camber came into its own to enable the deck to sustain the weight of the gasoline drums.

Everything reeked of gasoline. All day long the men breathed gasoline; the air that the ventilation circulated below decks was charged with gasoline; at mid-day the men were served gasoline-flavoured sandwiches and the water they drank tasted of gasoline.

It went without saying that smoking was forbidden; that was an order which the masters-at-arms had small trouble in enforcing, despite the misery and the grumbling that it aroused. Every man in the ship was on the side of enforcement in that atmosphere.

"But when's the smoking lamp going to be lit again?" asked Seaman First Class Malloy.

"One hour after the last drum goes over the side," answered Chief Bosun's Mate Trautmann.

"But—but——"

"That'll be the day after tomorrow," said Trautmann. "Maybe you can wait a couple of days. It'll do you good."

For this was the moment when the smokers on board began to feel their deprivation most acutely. The 208th drum had been brought on board, and Lieutenant Borglum had seen that it was secured into position and the two long lines of drums chocked and jammed absolutely tight. He had become aware that his captain had been unobtrusively overseeing the operation only when he made his report.

"Very well, Mr. Borglum, thank you," said Angell. "You have an hour to make up your sleep."

Borglum had had two nights without sleep, a day in Guadalcanal and a day dealing with gasoline drums. He was white and staring-eyed and glad to fall face downward in his bunk and sleep, despite the stifling heat and despite the convulsive memories of Guadalcanal that assailed him when he first lay down.

Boon went out into the growing night, leaving that pleasant anchorage behind, to emerge on to the endless Pacific and to start on her 500-mile journey from the New Hebrides to the Solomons. The long Pacific rollers were following her up with a speed hardly different from her own, so that her motion was strangely apathetic—a long sluggish climb, a prolonged levelling off and then a long descent, bows down.

And every time the stern rose and every time it fell, the rows of gasoline drums pressed against their chocks with a weight of nineteen tons on each side, first forward and then back, straining and compressing, gaining a millimeter of play in one direction and then two millimeters in the other, demanding the continual attention of Borglum and the carpenter's crew to wedge the masses back into rigidity before they took charge.

"I won't be sorry to get rid of this stuff, sir," said Chief Carpenter's Mate Macdonald.

"Neither shall I," agreed Borglum.

"Hard to think why a destroyer should be given a job like this, sir."

"No."

Borglum had been in Guadalcanal; he knew of the urgency there, about which the others could only form a vague mental picture. And nobody in the ship knew of the most cogent reason for the precarious balance of power here in the Southwest Pacific. Ten thousand miles away, on the other side of the globe, American might and American sea-power was bestirring itself. Under the guidance of a certain unknown General Eisenhower there was a hammer blow about to be struck. Operation Torch was being launched. A quarter of a million American soldiers and sailors were crossing the Atlantic, to tear North Africa from the grasp of Hitler and Mussolini.

Every available ship and man and gun and plane must be flung into Operation Torch, and on the opposite side of the world the barest minimum left to hold the Japanese. The barest minimum; that was why the Tokyo Express could come nightly rampaging down the Slot, and why the Marines held so precarious a foothold in Guadalcanal—and that was why *Boon* was heading there with a deckload of gasoline drums, a racehorse used as a packmule.

Northwestward she sped through the night, sometimes through deluges of rain, with squalls keeping almost exact pace with her so that her depressed stern and elevated blow caused her to react with pigheaded obstinacy to her helm before the following wind. Her sonar sounded the waters beneath her; her radar scanned the sky above and the surface ahead, and the lookouts strained their eyes to supplement these mechanical aids, for no man needed to be told that in the event of a battle *Boon* would be dreadfully handicapped and far more vulnerable even than usual.

Dawn brought the summons to general quarters; mid-day brought the fixing of the ship's position and the confirmation of Lieutenant Brown's original theory and subsequent suspicions that the following wind and the more efficient bite of the screws had set her some miles ahead of her reckoned position. Then in the afternoon there came a sudden appearance upon Lieutenant Klein's radar screen that sent him to the voice tube on the instant. It was the mountains of San Cristobal; *Boon* ran on steadily for nearly half an hour before the lookouts could pick them out, dark blue under their shrouding clouds, on the horizon over the starboard bow.

This was the first of the Solomons, the devil-haunted islands as the general had called them, and already Captain Angell was on the bridge ordering an alteration of course to three-five-five, and *Boon* heeled with a groaning of the deck cargo as she turned to enter the disputed area.

Now they were entering dangerous waters; they were entering into imminent peril. This was where the limits of sea power intersected. The two navies, straining like dogs on chains against the restrictions of lines of communication thousands of miles long, could just encounter each other here. First one and then the other could gather up it resources and make a spring forward and dominate these waters for a moment before the need for renewing supplies dragged them back again. The airborne sea power of the American carriers had won momentary control before damage to the *Enterprise* and *Saratoga* had shifted the balance. Now the Tokyo Express could come raging down the Slot as far as its fuel would allow, and Japanese planes, if the American planes allowed, could bomb everything in sight as far as this point—this point off the southeastern tip of Guadalcanal which *Boon* reached at sunset. During the night she would be comparatively safe from Japanese aerial attack.

"We'll be back here twelve hours from now," said Angell on the bridge.

"We'd better be, sir," said Brown. "Either that or we'll need damned good fighter cover."

"Yes," agreed Angell. He looked round. "See that the men are fed," he said. "Then you can sound general quarters."

"Aye aye, sir."

Boon ploughed along through the sudden darkness, with every nerve astrain now, with every man tense at his post. Klein at the radar screen reported the bearings to the bridge. Radar and sonar both picked up Nura to port.

"Course two-six-nine," ordered Angell.

"Course two-six-nine," repeated Flower, and *Boon* turned away from Malaita for Klein to pick up Rua Sura.

A report from a lookout. "Lights bearing two-five-zero. Gunfire, sir."

Now they could see it on the port bow, the battle of Guadalcanal, unending, unremitting, the momentary flashes of artillery and the prolonged gleam of flares.

Rua Sura dropped astern, and Sealark showed up ahead and the gun flashes swung round to *Boon*'s port beam as Angell directed the ship into Lengo Channel hardly a mile from the coast.

"All engines ahead one third. Make turns for four knots."

Boon's speed died away, but the most accurate estimate, the most acute navigation, was necessary to maintain an exact estimate of her position during the long moments while she carried her way before taking up her new speed. And now they were in touch by voice radio. Angell on *Boon*'s bridge could speak in person with the general on shore.

"We'll start dropping in five minutes' time, sir," reported Angell.

"Good. It's needed. You understand? It's needed."

"Yes, sir."

They could not be more explicit, when Japanese ears might be hearing the conversation. Angell spoke to the telephone talker.

"Fantail from bridge. Start dropping the drums."

Fifteen seconds' wait, and then a message back. "Bridge from fantail. Drums now being dropped."

In the darkness aft Borglum and his crew were pulling out the chocks from the drums, to be wheeled round and thrust over the timber chutes. Angell on the bridge could guess vaguely by the sounds at the progress of the work; he was better informed by a report from the talker.

"Bridge from fantail. Fifty drums dropped."

That was when Klein made a new report. He had disentangled something from the masses on the screen

34

representing Savo Island and Florida. He had seen sudden death approaching.

"Bridge! Skunk bearing three-one-three. Range seven thousand, closing."

Everyone on the bridge knew what that meant. The Tokyo Express was coming down the Slot.

"Six skunks. Three large, three small."

Three heavy cruisers and three destroyers, most likely, the usual sort of force that came down in the night hours to bombard the beaches and cover the landing of reinforcements. Eyes turned toward Angell. As Angell stepped to the TBS, the talker relayed a new report.

"Bridge from fantail. One hundred drums dropped."

Angell presumably heard; he was about to speak on the radio telephone to the general and did so without hesitation.

"Here's the Tokyo Express coming, sir," he said. "I'll be ready for action in three or four minutes."

The TBS squawked back at him. "Aye aye, sir," said Angell.

"Bridge from fantail. One hundred and fifty drums dropped."

"Bridge!" Klein was reporting. "Skunks bearing three-one-six. Range five thousand, closing."

"Bridge from fantail. Last drums going over."

"Sir," said Angell into the TBS, "I can go into action now. Surprise 'em."

As he spoke, a succession of brilliant gun flashes lighted the horizon on the starboard beam. The Japanese had opened their bombardment of Henderson Field. And the gunfire brought a flood of reports from the telephone talkers, now that the Japanese firing had revealed their presence to the *Boon*'s lookouts, "Bridge from fantail. All drums away."

Now the *Boon* could leap into action. Now she could wheel toward the Japanese, guns blazing, torpedo tubes training. She would go into her death, of course. The odds were too heavy. But she could deal more deadly blows; she could sink ten times her own tonnage before blazing ruin could overtake her. She could kill 3,000 Japanese while her own 300 died.

"Carry on with the duty assigned to you," squawked the general's voice, transformed by the TBS, into Angell's ear.

"All engines ahead full speed," snapped Angell, turning his head away from the radio telephone.

Boon leaped into life.

"Bridge from fire control. Request permission to open fire on surface target to starboard."

"Fire control from bridge. Permission not—repeat *not*—granted."

That was the first hint to the rest of the ship as to what the general had said to Angell, but nobody yet believed that *Boon* was going to evade a battle. All eyes were on Angell, waiting for him to put some daring and original plan into action. Out in Ironbottom Sound the Japanese guns were blazing, yet *Boon* held steadily on her course with no fresh orders to the helm; and the firing drew rapidly abaft the beam until she was heading directly away from her golden opportunity.

The Tokyo Express had the field to itself—was undisputed master of Ironbottom Sound, turning to east and to west in a succession of loops while raining shells on to the beaches and Henderson Field. For an hour the bombardment continued, and for an hour *Boon* slunk away from glory and death. Only at the end of an hour did Angell give a fresh order.

"All engines ahead one third."

That was all; no order was given to the helm, and *Boon* continued to head westward away from action, although at this diminished speed, while the gun flashes sank below the horizon and then reappeared as the Tokyo Express raged backward and forward.

At last a helm order from Angell. "Right standard rudder. Steady on course zero-nine-five."

That was the reciprocal of her previous course; *Boon* was coming back on her tracks, heading toward the Tokyo Express, but still at her laggard five knots. Then the firing ceased; there were no more gun flashes visible on the horizon ahead, and soon Klein's reports began to come in again. The Japanese ships were heading northwestward, homeward, up the Slot.

Angell applied himself to the radio-telephone; it was a matter of minutes before he was able to raise the general's headquarters again.

"We're starting to come down now, sir."

"Very well," squawked the TBS back at him; then there was a pause, apparently while the general listened to a newly-arrived report, and then general continued, "We're got eight so far. Looks as if the Nips did that much of your job for you. Thanks for what you've done, captain. And thanks for what you're going to do."

Angell turned from the TBS.

"All engines ahead flank speed."

Boon sprang into throbbing life again. As she gathered speed, Angell addressed himself to Brown.

"We'll have to shave Ringdove Shoal as close as we dare. We don't want to come down right through the drums."

"I was going to suggest that, sir."

"The general said they've got eight drums ashore already," said Angell to Brown. "It must have been the tail end of the wash from the Tokyo Express that put them ashore."

"Eight drums," repeated Brown, mostly to himself, and then, "That ought to fuel one plane anyway, sir. Can't say that I'm sure of the figures."

"We're going to send in another two hundred in the next five minutes," said Angell.

"Yes, sir." Brown paused before continuing. "It will be daylight in just over an hour, sir."

They could agree on it; they could do nothing about it.

"Another hour and a half at least after that before we're off Graham Point," Brown added.

"Yes."

The southeastern tip of Guadalcanal marked the limit of extreme range of the Japanese bombers. They would have a free run over *Boon* for a full hour and a half.

"I feel I don't care," said Angell suddenly. "What do you think the men think?"

"They'll be all right, sir," answered Brown. "They know. And we've been long enough together."

"I hope so."

38

Boon went racing down Lengo Channel. Invisible to her, the mountainous waves of her wake from her starboard side went out to burst in foam on the tortured shore of Guadalcanal—and the waves from her portside went out to be reflected back from Ringdove Shoal and Maxwell Shoal and to cross the channel again and help to sweep in the drums. There were marines, waist deep, shoulder deep, in the shallows, seizing the drums and wrestling them ashore, and on Henderson Field there were other marines working wildly in the darkness to transfer the contents of the drums to the tanks of the fighters.

Now *Boon* emerged from the shallows, retracing her course of the previous night, and Klein was reporting last night's landmarks just as before—Rua Sura and Nura and the mountains of Malaita. Then daylight suddenly began to illuminate the sky over Malaita.

"Right standard rudder. Steady on course one-five-four."

Boon wheeled round; she had only to maintain this course for a day to regain the shelter and the safety and the comfort of Espiritu Santo, and then came the alarm. Klein saw them in his screen, fifty miles away—but what was fifty miles to a squadron of Japanese bombers? A lone destroyer in Indispensable Strait would be easy prey for them, however skilfully her guns were manned, however cunningly her captain might twist and turn and manoeuvre.

"Bettys," said Angell, binoculars to his eyes. "Tell the engine room to make all the speed they can."

The men were at the guns, and *Boon* was flying at her highest speed southeastward for the safety that lay too far away. Dark against the blue of the sky the Japanese bombers swung in pursuit; *Boon* might as well have been standing still for all the use maximum speed would be to her.

"Bridge!" Klein's voice was urgent. "More bandits are coming! Bearing two-seven-five."

More enemies? The stifling air was already full of the sound of the Japanese engines, droning remorselessly louder and louder. Yet perhaps there was another note blending with it, something higher pitched, full of snarling menace.

"Bridge from fire control," said the monotonous voice of the talker, "request permission to open fire on air targets."

Out of the cloud they came, three of them, hurtling across the blue; on a converging course they were devouring the space between them and the bombers like ravening beasts. But a destroyer captain had to keep a clear head.

"Fire control from bridge." Angell's voice was steady. "Wait a minute."

"Look sir!" exclaimed Brown at that very moment. "Marines! They're F4F's."

It was machine-gun fire, not cannon fire, which was to deal death to the Japanese. The flat hammer sound of the firing came down from the blue to the listening ears in the *Boon*. The engines snarled and droned; planes swept in circles like the dancing of gnats; then there was the black smoke against the blue, a vertical streak of black, a white fountain of foam in the other blue of the sea, a spreading white circle with a smear of black smoke hovering over it. Another white fountain far more distant; the Japanese were flying for home; the clatter of the guns was almost inaudible.

Angell had not had to give the order to commence firing; the American planes had not had to take their chance with American gunfire.

"All engines ahead full," said Captain Angell.

A destroyer captain has to remember everything; he has to think of fuel consumption and of the wear and tear on engines driven at maximum speed; he has to remember this despite his feeling of relief, despite every reaction from tension. Despite, too, all the other thoughts flooding his mind. The general on Guadalcanal must be a man of vision as well as a man of resolution. He must have worked out in his mind where *Boon* would be at dawn; he must have thought about her vulnerability, and he must have taken an early decision to send his first fighter patrol in that direction, both to protect her and to destroy the enemy her presence would attract.

"Here's an F4F coming back, sir," reported Brown.

It came winging down toward the *Boon*, and Angell could speak to the pilot, thanks to Klein's radiomen, who had been able to tune their one remaining transmitter-receiver to the fighter-director frequency.

"Thank you," he said.

"You're more than welcome, pal," squawked the radio in reply. "Glad to be of service any time. Any time that you bring us the gas."

Angell replaced the hand set and watched the

fighter heading back to Guadalcanal. He still had his
duties to do, his ship to think about.

"Secure from general quarters," he ordered, and
then he remembered something else. "The smoking
lamp can be lit now."

The Boy Stood on the Burning Deck

In this story his name is Ed Jones; his real name is completely different from that. He runs a filling station near where I live, and I often buy gas there; his is not a calling that promises high adventure, nor is it likely to demand selfless devotion to duty. Just after the war the crossroads was quite a lonely point, and Ed's filling station was the only building within half a mile. With the population shift into California there are now great tracts of houses within sight, and there are rows of markets and shops. One might expect in consequence that Ed has made a fortune, but now each of the four corners of the crossroads is occupied by a filling station, and there are plenty of others not far away. Ed agrees that he makes twice as much money as he did when he came here, after his discharge from the Navy; but he points out philosophically that he can buy with his doubled income no more than he could before, and he works four times as hard to earn it.

But I want to write about Ed Jones, and not about his filling station; he is the more interesting subject. I have known him for all these years, and I have always liked him, and his sturdy wife Mary, and the four postwar children whom I have seen growing up from babyhood. And I have used the name Ed Jones not only because it is unlike his real one but because it does not suggest heroism or self-sacrifice; neither does he himself—I might otherwise have called him Ironside or Strong. I knew he had served in the Navy during the war, but it was only recently that it came out in casual conversation that he had served in the destroyer *Boon*, and my interest was caught at once, because I have been writing stories about the *Boon*. I did my best to induce him to talk, but without any great success; Ed is not a very communicative man.

It did not call for any great degree of cunning to enlist the services of Mary, his wife. She was on my side almost from the start, but even her coaxing achieved little. Ed only laughed when he did not shrug his shoulders. Then one day when I was about to drive away Mary put her head in at my car window —it was one of the moments (and there are plenty of them) when she looks twenty rather than forty.

"I still have all the letters that he wrote me during the war," she said, breathlessly.

"That's just the sort of thing I'm after," I said. "Are you going to let me read them?"

"Hey, hold on a minute," interposed Ed. "Those letters—you know—they're not—"

"They're twenty years old," protested Mary. "And there's nothing to be ashamed of. And—" she turned back to me—"you wouldn't—"

"I wouldn't read anything I wasn't supposed to read," I said. "I'm pretty good at that. I expect they were most of them read by a censor at some time or other, anyway."

That was how it happened that one evening I found myself sitting in the Jones's house with a cup of coffee at my elbow, and the sound of the television turned down to the lowest limit the children would tolerate, while Mary brought me the letters. She blushed quite charmingly, with a gesture to excuse the sentiment of a young bride who had tied the letters up in pink ribbons (faded now) and packed them in a heart-shaped box which had presumably once held a Valentine's Day gift of chocolates.

To a man who deals with history letters contemporary with the events he is studying are frequently valuable material. Accounts written later are usually coloured by the knowledge of what actually happened, and are distorted by later prejudices and legends. Wartime letters may be distorted too, admittedly, through the necessity of obeying wartime censorship regulations, and also because husbands and wives often wished to appear more cheerful than they actually were. But even the letters that are distorted badly convey an atmosphere, a mood, that is hard to recapture otherwise, and which is important when reconstructing a period; and sometimes they at least give clues that lead to the unearthing of forgotten facts.

"Thank you, Mary," I said, and shot a glance at Ed before beginning to read; he appeared to have all his attention concentrated upon television.

The letters were love letters, naturally; from the first they contained much of what might be expected to be written by a young sailor who had newly joined the Navy and was newly separated from his young bride. My eye ran rapidly down paragraphs that had

45

little bearing on the war, trying not to read the tender passages while making sure there was no history buried in them. The letters were all dated and in sequence, and as I read I was conscious of a feeling that I could see into the future, that I had a Cassandra-like ability to prophesy. The letter of December 6th, 1941, written from machinist's mates' strikers school, had a light-hearted gaiety that I knew could not endure; and I was ridiculously pleased with myself as though I had really achieved something, when the next letter, of December 8th, written after Pearl Harbor, confirmed my feeling.

It was interesting to read how Fireman Third Class Jones reacted to that news. The earlier letters had breathed a certain patriotism, whose sincerity could be guessed at despite the writer's difficulty in expressing it; this new letter told of a hardened resolve, of a grimmer determination, and it was easy to read into it the writer's certainty that every recruit around him felt similarly inspired. That was an historical fact.

"You don't have to read them if they're not what you want, you know," said Mary.

"You couldn't stop me," I answered, reaching for the next letter.

I still felt like Cassandra as I read on; when Fireman Second Class Jones wrote that he was being transferred out of training center and wondered what was going to happen next I knew that he was going to the *Boon*, and so he was—here was his new Fleet Post Office address to prove it. And when he speculated regarding where *Boon* would be sent, I already knew. I could not merely follow him and the

Boon across the Pacific and back again—I could travel ahead of them. There were things I knew about which only showed up vaguely in the letters, thanks to the censorship. I knew about the torpedoing of the Japanese cruiser, and I knew about the rescuing of the navy pilot in his rubber boat ten days after the battle of the Coral Sea, and I knew, although Fireman First Class Jones did not, that the *Boon* was going to be one of the ships transferred back to Pearl Harbor to meet the next Japanese thrust, the one that ended in Japanese disaster at Midway. I was conscious of a quickening of the pulse as I reached for the next letter. I wanted to know about Midway, and how the *Boon* comported herself there. The accounts of the battle are so taken up with the action of the carriers, and with the attacks and counter-attacks launched by the aircraft, that there is nothing to spare for an insignificant destroyer like the *Boon*. I wanted to know how much the lower deck knew about the battle; how conscious the men were of having taken part in one of the decisive battles of the war; there was so much I wanted to know. And here was the next letter, just the top and bottom of it, connected by a thin thread of paper, with all the middle of it cut out by the censor's scissors. My keen anticipation was replaced by a dull disappointment. There it was. Fireman First Class Jones had been promoted to Machinist's Mate Second Class—and then this gap. Some of it I could fill. Jones's rapid promotion was proof of his reliability and of the good opinion which his officers held of him; it was also an indication of the rapid expansion of the United States Navy. Clearly on arrival at Pearl there had been considerable transfers of personnel—skilled ratings had been taken out to help man the flood of new construction. Fresh recruits had been put on board and the gaps among the petty officers had been filled by promotions. I could be quite sure of this; but what had *Boon* achieved in the battle? What had been Jones's experiences? I broke in upon his contemplation of television.

"What happened here?" I asked, calling his attention to the gap in the letter. He had to look at it twice before he could be sure which letter it was.

"Oh, that?" he said. "I didn't know they'd cut all that out of that letter. I wrote that from the sick bay at Pearl."

"So I see," I said. "How did you get there? What happened?"

He told me in the end, neither willingly nor fluently. To a reader that long-drawn interchange of question and answer would be tedious, no doubt. This is the tale of what happened; this is the completed picture, put together as though Jones's halting answers to my questions were the pieces of a jigsaw puzzle, but with nothing else added.

Machinist's Mate Second Class Ed Jones had the duty, at General Quarters, of attending to the throttle of the port engine in the *Boon*. He stood on a restricted area of iron deck down in the engine room with the wheel of the valve in his hands and an instrument board on the bulkhead before him. Turning the wheel to the right reduced the amount of steam admitted to the turbine from the boilers; turning to the left increased it, and of course the speed of the turbine—and hence of the port propeller—varied in proportion. On the board in front of him appeared repetitions of the signals from the bridge regarding speed, the five speeds ahead and the three speeds astern and stop. By reference to the tachometer there he could adjust the speed of revolution of the turbine in accordance with the demands made upon him; the control was sensitive enough for him to be able to produce almost exactly any number of revolutions required. And on the board was the dial of another tachometer as well, which registered the revolutions of the starboard engine, and it was Jones's business to see that the two readings agreed.

So during battle that was where he stood, hands on the wheel, adjusting carefully to left or to right, or spinning hurriedly when a large change of speed was ordered; a very solitary and usually monotonous job that demanded unflagging attention. A critic might suggest that all this could be as well done, or better, by a machine; an apparatus that would respond automatically to the signals from the bridge and to the readings of the tachometers. That is perfectly true—such an apparatus would be absurdly simple compared with many employed in ships of war. But that was the real point; this was a ship of war, and the regulation of the flow of steam was a vital function, one of overwhelming importance. A shell fragment or a near miss could put such an apparatus out of action easily enough, and that would be a disaster—there would be nothing to replace it. Naturally a shell fragment could put the human operator out of action too, but that would not be such a disaster. Once his dead body had been dragged out of the way another man could take his place.

Boon took her way out from Pearl Harbor along with the two carrier task forces which were going to fight the battle. She was part of the screen, naturally, part of the tight ring thrown about the vital carriers to protect them as much as possible from submarine and air attack. The tighter the ring the more efficient the protection and the greater the demand for good seamanship. The carriers had to make extravagant turns into the wind to fly off their planes and to fly them on again, and then the screen had to dash madly in far wider arcs to maintain their covering positions; there was fuelling at sea to be carried out, pilots to be rescued. A very small miscalculation could mean a collision and disaster. So could a very small mistake by Jones. The best of captains on the bridge could only watch, helpless, as catastrophe loomed ahead, if Jones in an absent-minded moment spun that wheel the wrong way or did not pay instant attention to the captain's signals.

Boon had hardly secured from General Quarters after sunrise on that historic morning when the warnings sounded again and the men had to go back to their battle stations.

"Did you expect a battle?" I asked, when Jones reached this point in his answers to my questions.

"Oh yes," said Jones. His tone echoed the fatalism of the man under orders, or perhaps the steady determination of the man with a duty to perform.

"So what happened then?"

Jones ran down below, down the iron ladders, to his station at the throttle valve. He experienced a momentary regret as he did so, for on deck it was a beautiful day of sunshine and occasional cloud, just warm enough and delightful. He wished that fate had made him a gunner at one of the 20 mm guns, so that he could stay topside and enjoy it. His battle station was too brightly lit to be called gloomy, but it was stark and inhospitable and lonely. He stood there with the steel deck gently swaying under his feet, busy enough after a few moments when the bridge signalled for revolutions for 25 knots—about as fast as the old *Boon* could go without straining herself—and then for repeated small variations to keep her in her station screening the carrier. The speed itself, with the old destroyer vibrating and trembling, was enough to make Jones quite certain that action was impending, but he knew nothing more than that. He could only stand there, watching his instrument board and moving his wheel, while the fate of the civilised world—of the uncivilised world as well—was being decided over his head. He knew nothing of the Japanese carrier force far away over the horizon, of the fleets of planes soaring into the air and returning, of the fighters wheeling overhead maintaining combat air patrol high up in the blue. He could not guess at the decisions that were being reached by the admirals—decisions that might determine his immediate death or survival, but which would affect his whole future life, even if he lived on to old age as a civilian.

He knew nothing of how the Japanese admirals had been tempted into delivering a blow at Midway, so that they were caught off guard by the sudden unexpected appearance of the American carriers within striking distance of their own. The hours went by for Jones in solitary monotony while death rained down on Midway and the bombers from Midway went in to heroic death round the Japanese carriers, and while the planes from his own task force avenged them a hundredfold in a new surprise attack. Jones knew almost nothing of what was going on; the breaks in the monotony—the only indications that the task force was engaged in operations—were the occasional sudden turns, when the *Boon* lay over, without warning, under full rudder. When she did that Jones might well have lost his footing, but he was an experienced seaman by now, and he could steady himself by his hands that gripped the wheel, although even then he sorely wrenched himself in his efforts to combat the sudden inclinations. These told him, however, that the task force was flying planes on and off and that the screen was having to wheel about to shelter the carrier.

Then the monotony was abruptly broken in a new way. Every gun the *Boon* carried suddenly began to fire. The loud bangs of the 5-inch and the earsplitting cracks of the small calibres were carried by the fabric of the ship direct, it almost appeared, to a focus in the steel cell where Jones stood. The concentrated noise was frightful, and the deck on which he stood and the wheel which he held in his hands leaped and vibrated with the concussions, and it seemed as if every five seconds the ship was making a radical alteration of course, lying over madly first one way and then the other, so rapidly and unexpectedly that this, combined with the vibrations, came nearer than ever before to sweeping him off his feet.

He could guess perfectly well what was going on. The suddenness with which it all began, the fact that the small guns were firing as well as the large ones, and the constant alterations of course, told him that they were under air attack. Any other kind of daylight battle would have developed more slowly and the small calibre guns would not have opened fire as yet, while if they were hunting a submarine the guns would not be firing at all, most likely, and certainly not for so long continuously. Being under air attack made no difference to his circumstances; all he had to do still was to attend to his signals and tachometers, and regulate his valve.

The destiny of the world was being decided over his head; the Japanese carrier planes had at last discovered the presence of the task force and were hurtling in to the attack. They were coming in with the speed and skill developed in years of training; their pilots were displaying the courage of their race; some of them more reckless even than usual, for they knew of the disasters that had befallen some of their own carriers and were frantic for revenge—frantic with desperation, some of them, for they guessed that their sinking carriers could no longer provide them with a refuge, so that the pilots' lives at longest could be measured by the gasoline in their tanks.

Suddenly it appeared to Jones as if the *Boon* had leaped clear out of the sea, as if his feet were pressing like ton weights upon the deck beneath them, and as if his thighs were being driven into his body, and then the deck fell away beneath him and the *Boon* rolled and pitched and plunged so that once more only his grip on the wheel saved him from being flung down. He knew, of course, what had caused all this. It was the near miss, the bomb bursting close

53

alongside, which to this day is coldly recorded in the statistical accounts of the battle. It left the *Boon* strained and buckled although she could still steam and still fight and still cover the aircraft carrier she had to guard with her life. Jones knew that she was strained and buckled—he had cautiously to shift position to keep his footing, and, looking down, he could see that the steel plate on which he stood was inclined slightly upwards from one edge, where it had torn free from its weld to its neighbour, leaving a gap, and it threatened to part altogether and drop him down into the bilges below.

But he could not think about that; his tachometer was registering a declining number of revolutions and he had to spin the wheel hurriedly to bring it back to its proper figure, even while his brain told him that the boiler room must have suffered damage so that the steam pressure had fallen. Not even that deduction had full time to mature. Even as he was thinking along these lines a new hellish noise burst round him. Wango—wango—wango—but much faster than human lips could enunciate those sounds. Some low flying torpedo plane, its torpedo launched, was doing what further damage it could, and had opened fire with its machine guns. The bullets beat upon the thin steel plates; the heavy calibre ones came clean through and the tracers set the *Boon* on fire. To Jones those seconds were like being in an iron pipe while a dozen men pounded the outside with hammers, but it was only a matter of seconds. The tachometer was behaving erratically, echoing what was going on in the boiler room, and he had to work hard on the valve to keep it steady.

Then the *Boon* lay over again in another desperate turn, and he became aware of a fresh complication. There was a rush of flame up through the gaps in the plating on which he stood, flames licking knee-high around him. He had to shrink to one side to avoid them, and then, as the *Boon* steadied herself on her new course, they died down leaving only a red glow below. The *Boon* lay over again, and the flames lifted their heads again. A ruptured fuel tank had leaked some of its contents into the bilges, and the oil had been set on fire. With the motion of the ship the flaming oil was washing back and forth under Jones's feet, rising higher towards him as the *Boon* turned. Amid the continuous din of the guns Jones was being roasted over an intermittent fire.

Yet whether *Boon* was turning or not, there was still some fire below him; the iron deck on which Jones stood was growing hotter and hotter. Amid the varied stinks that filled the engine room Jones noticed a new one—the acrid smell of burning leather, and at the same time he was conscious of agony in the soles of his feet. The worn-out old shoes that he kept for wear in the engine room were charring against the hot iron. He took his hands from the valve long enough to tear off his outer clothing, and he trampled that under his feet to insulate them from the plating, kicking off the smouldering shoes. That gave him a momentary respite, but momentary only. Soon his jumper and trousers were smouldering too, as he stood on them. He was leaping with the pain.

"What about damage control?" I asked.

"They'd had a lot of casualties," explained Jones. "And there were plenty of other fires to put out, too."

"How long did this go on?"

"Oh, I don't know. Long enough."

The guns were silent by now, for the Japanese planes had gone, the pilots to their deaths. *Akagi* and *Kaga*, *Hiryu* and *Soryu*, the four proud Japanese carriers, were sunk or sinking, and the battle of Midway was won. The *Boon* lay over once more, as she turned to help pick up survivors from the sinking *Yorktown*, and Jones was momentarily bathed in flames again. And then came the signal from the bridge.

"Stop."

Jones spun the wheel as his tortured feet charred on the hot plating, and then down the ladder came clattering the damage control party. It was only a matter of moments for the foam to extinguish the flames in the bilges, and even a brief spraying from a hose cooled the twisted plating on which Jones stood. Nor did he have to bear the agony of standing much longer, for he asked for, and obtained, a relief. He was a vigorous and athletic young man, and he was able to go up the ladder hand over hand without torturing himself further by putting his burned feet on the rungs, and then he could crawl on hands and knees along the deck for a little way before he collapsed. And the task force returned victorious to Pearl Harbor, and *Boon* went into dry dock, and Jones went into the hospital.

"Didn't anybody ask you how your feet got burned?" I asked.

"Not specially. A lot of fellows got burns that day. Worse than mine," said Jones.

"What about this?" I went on, indicating the mutilated letter.

"Oh, of course I wrote to Mary. I wanted to tell her how I'd come to be in the hospital, naturally, and I suppose they cut it out."

I could picture that part quite well; the weary officer with a hundred letters to censor, reading a description of the flaming bilges of the *Boon*. The damage had not been announced, and this was censorable material. He would take his scissors and cut out the offending passage. His brain would be too numb to think much about the heroism written between the lines of that passage; or perhaps he took heroism for granted.

Now I have told the story. One of the best-known pieces of verse in the English language tells of a boy standing on a burning deck; I can only write a short story. Of course, in addition, I can go on buying gasoline from Ed Jones.

Dr. Blanke's First Command

Malcolm Blanke, M.D., was in a state of mental turmoil when he came back into the room where he had undergone his oral examination. Two stupendous things were happening to him at once. He was about to learn if he was to be granted a Ph.D., and he had just joined the United States Navy. About the Ph.D. he would hardly have worried at all if that had been the only factor in his present life. He had every confidence in his thesis on the Histology of the Peripheral Neural Plexuses.

It had broken new ground; it had disproved one theory and established another, and it opened the way to a fresh series of important researches. It had called for four years of hard work—four years of the most slavish concentration, the most accurate laboratory technique, the most painstaking observations and the most ingenious theorising regarding the deductions to be made from them. The examining board could hardly deny him his Ph.D. now that they had studied his thesis.

Incidentally, it was more than likely that the end result of his work would be the alleviation of a good deal of human suffering, which was a strange thought in a world at war—Blanke could think that way now that he was emerging from four years of total abstraction and now that he had joined the Navy. In fact, as he went back into the room to hear the decision of the examining board regarding his Ph.D., another absurd human thought came up into his mind—at some rare frivolous moment in his youth he had read about the procedure at Naval courts-martial, and how the accused, coming in to be told the finding, was warned in advance by the position of his sword on the table; the sword point toward him meant a verdict of guilty. Blanke remembered this as he remembered everything he had ever read because he had the fantastic memory of the true scholar, but the clearest proof that he had been jolted out of a purely academic state of mind was that he actually found himself sparing a glance at the council table to see if there was a sword there.

"I must offer you my heartiest congratulations on your thesis, Doctor Blanke," said the chairman of the examining board.

"A very definite contribution to human knowledge," said another member.

"Thank you, sir. Thank you," said Blanke vaguely in acknowledgement.

"I understand we should address you as Lieutenant Blanke, and not as Doctor Blanke, in the future," remarked the chairman.

"I suppose that's so," agreed Blanke. "I've just received my orders."

"At any rate, you have your Ph.D.," said the chairman, "but I don't expect it will be much use to you in the Navy. Undoubtedly it's your medical degree that interests Uncle Sam at the present time."

The day the last word of the thesis had been typed, the last reference checked, Blanke had sent in his application to join the Navy. Less than a week later the Navy had asked for a copy of his M.D. degree, something he had almost forgotten about during four years of research. And now he was a lieutenant (j.g.) USNR—for years, he knew, that would be far more important than just being a Ph.D.

He went back to his home, and his mother awaited him as he let himself in at the door. She was Doctor Blanke, the same as he was; her vocation had been mathematics, but she had years ago reconciled herself to the fact that her son had chosen to be a mere scientist.

"Well, dear?" she said.

"It's all right, mother."

"I'm glad, dear," she said. "Of course, I never had any doubts."

She might have been expected to discuss his Ph.D. further, but she was a woman as well as a Doctor of Philosophy, and there was something else she could hardly wait to mention.

"There are about a dozen big packages for you, dear," she said.

"My uniforms, I expect," Blanke said.

"Well, aren't you going to open them?" demanded his exasperated mother.

"Of course I will, mother," said he. "In fact, I seem to have heard somewhere that it's illegal for a member of the armed forces to wear civilian clothes now that there's a war."

"I'll help you, dear," said his mother.

Over some of the packages there was a shade of

disappointment. "You didn't need any more under-clothes, did you, dear?" asked his mother.

Blanke came over and looked at the contents. "That," he decided, "must be the 'six undershirts and six pairs of drawers' they spoke about."

"Your present things are much more suitable," sniffed his mother.

"Here's the khaki," said Blanke, opening another package. He unfolded the coat and held it up for inspection.

"Don't you think you'd better try it on, dear?" said his mother.

She left him while he put on regulation shirt and coat and trousers and tied the regulation tie. When he called her in again, he was standing before the mirror, trying to appear unconcerned at the first sight of himself in uniform.

"You look quite handsome, dear," she said, and only a mother could have thought that the gangling Blanke, with his laboratory pallor and scholarly shoulders, was "quite handsome." Blanke turned back to the mirror.

"Just a minute," said his mother, diving into one of the packages. "Here's something else you have to have." She produced the shoulder boards with their gold stripes.

"Yes, of course," agreed Blanke. "They show my rank. Let's put 'em on."

He buttoned them on his shoulders, and his mother handed him the regulation Navy cap. Blanke did not find much reassurance in the reflection that stared back at him out of the mirror. The United States Navy cap of 1942 did not sit well over a long, intellectual face; the coat was startlingly new and did not fit him very well. A more objective eye than Blanke's or his mother's would have thought he looked less like a Naval officer than like a scarecrow that had oddly acquired a new Naval uniform.

To be out in the street was a little disturbing; it seemed as if every eye were on him, even though he assured himself that by now Naval officers were common enough to attract no notice. After he dismounted from the bus in the vicinity of the Naval District Headquarters, he realised that uniformed men were saluting him as they passed. As he entered the doors, he wondered if he should take off his cap. He knew that the Navy had odd customs to which he would have to conform, so he drew himself up to the full height of his gangling six feet three and spoke stiffly down to seaman's stocky five feet four in what he decided was a peculiarly inefficient way of asking where he could find the transportation officer.

He said, "Thank you"—surely Naval discipline did not ban that minor politeness—and turned away to follow the instructions given him. And then he entered into an encounter which was, in time to come, to save his life and the lives of fifty other men. A burly figure in khaki had intercepted him.

"Excuse me, sir."

"Yes?" asked Blanke.

"Could you spare me a minute before you go to the transportation desk, sir?"

"Yes, I suppose so." Blanke remembered to look at the shoulder boards; these were decorated each with a thin band of alternate blue and gold, and Blanke had no idea what rank this indicated, but he was reassured by the fact that he was being addressed as "sir," even though the man who spoke to him had snow-white hair. This individual looked around as if considering what action to take.

"This way, sir," he said, making up his mind. He led Blanke to a small office at the side of the entrance hall, and at a jerk of his thumb the three seamen sitting there at desks got up and left. When the door closed behind them, Blanke found himself being looked at with a sort of kindly forbearance that puzzled him.

"You've just joined, sir?"

"Yes."

"You haven't been to indoctrination school yet?"

"No," replied Blanke, who had never even heard of indoctrination school.

"Are you on your way there, sir?"

"No. I'm going to join my ship."

"Your ship, sir!" The astonishment was profound. "Well, you must excuse me, sir, but you can't go there like that."

"Why, what's wrong?"

"Everything, sir, if you'll excuse me. Those shoulder boards. You're wearing 'em the wrong way round, sir. You should have the points inward so the stripes aren't up under your neck. Here, let me do it for you, sir . . . That's better. And these buttons—you keep them done up, all the time. And the pocket flaps should be out, not in."

By the time everything had been twitched into position, even Blanke was aware of the improvement.

"Thank you," he said with genuine gratitude. He knew he had much to learn, and this would be as good a time to start as any. "Who is it I'm thanking?"

"Warrant bo'sun, sir. Warrant Bosun Dean. Thirty-seven years' service, but they won't let me go to sea now. You don't mind me speaking to you like this, sir?"

"Mind? I'm grateful to you, of course. I have to learn sometime."

"It's too bad they're sending you to sea without any indoctrination at all. But I know they're short of doctors. What ship, sir?"

Blanke had to stop and think, for one name meant no more to him than another. "The *Boon*."

"*Boon?* DD."

"DD?"

"Destroyer, sir."

Dean tried to conceal the pity he felt for a man who did not know what a "DD" meant and yet was going to be pitchforked into one.

"That's one of the smaller ships, I take it," said Blanke.

"You're darn right, sir," agreed Dean. "Let me show you the way to the transportation desk."

Blanke was learning fast; when he arrived at the desk he was much relieved that the glance the transportation officer gave him was very different from the glances he had received so far. He was looked at as if he were just one more raw lieutenant in the medical corps, and that was an immense step upward.

"Priority Four," said the transportation officer, examining Blanke's orders. "You could be here for weeks if we try to fly you out. But you've got to go. They want doctors."

He opened first one file and then another and ran

through them without result. Then another idea struck him, and he reached for a third file.

"That's it," he said. "We can kill two birds with one stone. You're ready to go on board, I suppose?"

"Well, yes," said Blanke.

"Tonight?"

"Of course, if it's necessary."

"It's necessary, all right. *Wilhelmina*—Dutch registry, chartered transport, Dutch officers, Javanese crew. She's taking an anti-aircraft artillery outfit out to Nouméa. They haven't an Army doctor with them, and we can fit you in all right. I'll get your orders endorsed. Come back in ten minutes."

Blanke walked away a little dazed, but trying to appear as if he were perfectly accustomed to being ordered to sail at a moment's notice with a Javanese crew to a place he had never heard of. He was grateful when bosun Dean appeared.

"Did they give you any orders, sir?" he asked, and Blanke told him. "*Wilhelmina*. She's a fast transport—one of the ships that got away when the Japs overran the Dutch East Indies. Look here, sir, would you care to come and wait in my office while they type out your orders?"

Blanke was glad to accept, was glad to take the proffered chair and the proffered cigarette. The transition was continuing. The eagle powers of observation that for four years had expended themselves down the tube of a microscope were beginning to devote themselves now to the human beings and the material things that constituted his new world. He was aware of the concern, almost paternal, with which Dean was regarding him.

"It's only now that they've decided to put doctors into every destroyer, sir," explained Dean. "Only one in four in peacetime. But now the DD's have twice as many men on board. And those ships fight—more likely to fight than the battle wagons are."

"I see," said Blanke.

He would have to study the technique of naval warfare—and make plans how best to give rapid care to a crowd of wounded men in a shell-torn steel hull. Dean was shaking his head with something of sorrow —no, sympathy—in his expression.

"You don't know *anything*, do you, sir?" he said.

"I'm afraid I don't. I'll have to do some reading."

"I wish we was going to be in the same ship, sir," said Dean. "I could teach you a lot, quick."

"I wish we were," said Blanke with sincerity.

Dean's eyes strayed to something on the desk before him. Then he took the plunge.

"Look, Doc," he said. "I won't have the chance to make a Navy man out of you, but here's a book. Take it and learn something about the Navy." It was a largish, bluebound book that he offered.

"That's very kind of you," said Blanke, taking it; he did not know yet that his life depended on his taking it. It was the *Bluejacket's Manual,* and as he ran through the pages, all sorts of headings met his eye—"Uniform Regulations," "Types of Navy Ships," "Routines Aboard Ship" and more advanced subjects, like "Communications and Signalling" and "Boat Seamanship."

"Thank you again," said Blanke. "This must be just what I need."

"You're very welcome," said Dean. "I hope you

find it useful. You'll have plenty of time for reading in the *Wilhelmina*—and your orders'll be ready by now, I expect, sir."

Those orders took Blanke on board the *Wilhelmina* that night. He walked down the gangway on to the first deck—except for ferryboats—that he had ever trodden in his life. There were soldiers and packing cases everywhere. Someone with dark skin—Javanese, Blanke guessed—passed him on to a harassed individual who said, "Dis vay, pliss" and led him to a cabin where a fat Dutchman in shirt sleeves sat at a desk and read Blanke's orders and groaned.

"O.K.," he said at length. "You slip here."

"Here?"

The little cabin seemed to be completely full, with a desk and a bed and miscellaneous packages, but a wave of the fat Dutchman's arm indicated that there was an upper bed against the wall.

"I'm de purser," said the fat man. "I slip here." He indicated the lower bed, then said, "I am busy."

Blanke went quietly, nor was he averse to seeing something more of this first ship of his. As he entered a corridor, a door opened, revealing an Army officer who noticed his uniform and politely stood by the door for him to enter. It was a small room full of tobacco smoke and crowded with men who made him welcome and introduced themselves, the officers of the anti-aircraft unit whose enlisted men thronged the deck.

"Glad to find we have a doctor with us after all," said one of the captains, and Blanke forebore to comment on the remark.

He was content to sit silent, for the officers, he was glad to observe, were as excited as he was and soon left him out of the conversation when he offered no contribution to it. After a time one of the lieutenants, at a nod from one of the captains, left for the purpose, as he said, of "seeing the boys into bed." Blanke saw his opportunity to say good night, made his way back by a miracle to the purser's cabin and entered it to find the purser stretched out on the lower bed, still checking through papers and not in the least inclined to conversation.

Blanke discovered how to lower his bed, just as he would have found out the principle of some novel piece of laboratory apparatus, and he climbed up and in. He glanced at the three books he had taken to bed with him, put down the *Bluejacket's Manual*, picked up and discarded *Wounds and Burns*, did the same with *Preventive Medicine in Tropical Climates*, and went back to the *Bluejacket's Manual* again. He was tired enough to go to sleep quite shortly, with the light on and the *Bluejacket's Manual* on his chest.

So it was in this way that Malcolm Blanke went to sea for the first time, a queer introduction to Naval life, and yet one that early enough made plain to him the salient characteristics of life at sea in wartime—monotony, overcrowding, lack of privacy. In the *Wilhelmina* the United States officers shared the quarters of the Dutch officers, which meant that three men lived where one lived before; the sergeants shared with the ship's bosun and the stewards, about four men to one prewar berth, while the soldiers, 200 of them, could spread themselves where twelve passengers had once lived in comfort. And through all this the Javanese crew flitted like ghosts, going about the ship's business as if all these others did not exist.

There was little to do; there was very little that could be done in those cramped conditions. Twice a day there was boat drill and abandon-ship drill; there was physical drill; there were classes in the theory of anti-aircraft gunnery, and not even the blue Pacific sky could brighten those. For twenty-four hours the prospect of arriving at the romantic Hawaiian Islands lifted the pall of boredom, but the pall closed down all the thicker when the *Wilhelmina* steamed out again into the endless Pacific after only eighteen hours' stay, during which not a soldier set foot on shore.

The one man in the ship who was free of boredom was, naturally, Blanke. He was a true scholar, and here he was congenially employed in study; and the tasks he set himself had the unusual quality of being planned for practical ends. He had to make himself ready for a new life; there would be fantastic demands made upon him, and he had to prepare himself to meet them. With the intense concentration of a scholar, he read the books he had with him; to achieve that concentration he spent most of his time stretched out in the upper berth of the purser's cabin, for the purser was a man of few words who left him alone and allowed him a privacy impossible to find in the crowded wardroom or on the noisy deck. He read his professional books with care, calling up memories of his life as a hospital intern to fill in the gaps. He would lay his book down, gaze up at the deck beams overhead and take himself, step by step, through an emergency appendectomy, for instance.

That was easier than trying to picture himself handling casualties in a destroyer under fire, but he rigorously made himself visualise those possible situations as well.

Naturally he was methodical about all this; no one without method could have devised the scheme of research which had resulted in his Ph.D. thesis. He spent his mornings in study of his professional books, with a break for sick call, which he attended at the request of the officer commanding the troops, but at which nothing ever showed up which could not have been safely left to the medical corporal. Two hours in the afternoon he devoted to acquiring a tan, with nicely judged proportions of shade and sunshine, because he knew he would be much exposed to tropical suns in the future. And the rest of his time he read the *Bluejacket's Manual,* and this was the hardest work of his day. It called for an effort of will to concentrate on the thousands of new facts presented in those 800 crowded pages. But he made himself learn them, conscientiously setting himself to answer the quizzes at the ends of the chapters to test his knowledge.

Some of the knowledge was obviously advantageous; he learned about specialty marks and insignia, and in the few moments when he could be alone, he taught himself to salute in the prescribed method. He read about Personal Hygiene and First Aid to inform himself about what the Navy thought officially about these things; that was easier than the Manual of Arms and Close Order Drill, but he worked through those before applying himself to the more interesting chapters on Types of Navy Ships and Shipboard Routine. It was hard to study the technique of

Cleaning and Painting, but the General Safety Precautions, of course, had a direct bearing on his future duties. He read everything and he conscientiously stored everything away in his remarkable memory. When he reached the glossary at the end, and admitted to himself that he knew the meaning of every term in it, from "abaft" to "yoke", he felt an actual sense of loss in that he had no further difficult work to occupy his mind—and the *Wilhelmina* was still not due to arrive at Nouméa for another four days.

That was when tragedy struck; that was when Blanke learned that those long periods of tedium that characterise Naval life in wartime can be terminated in a single second.

Blanke was in his bunk dozing, his open book on his chest, when the torpedo exploded. He woke, only conscious that something violent had happened. The thundering noise he heard next second he could not explain to himself; it was the sound of the water, flung hundreds of feet into the air, bursting over the upper works of the *Wilhelmina*. Then there was a momentary silence, a dead, dead silence, in the midst of which the *Wilhelmina* lay suddenly over toward one side, rolling him against the bulkhead. He found the light switch and pressed it, and there was no result; he clicked it twice more before he realised that the electric power was off. Down below him the purser was talking volubly yet quietly in Dutch, and then Blanke heard a whistle blowing outside, its staccato notes bearing a message of great urgency.

He knew now that the *Wilhelmina* had been torpedoed, that she was lying helpless, without power, without even steam for the siren, and that she was heeling over in her death agony. He hauled himself up against the list out of bed. Those urgent whistle notes outside conveyed something of panic, and for two or three seconds that panic infected him; he was blundering frantically in the darkness of the cabin before he pulled himself together. He had learned by painful experience in the laboratory and operating theatre that haste and carelessness brought disaster—that reaction came fast, and pride came only second. He was the only Naval officer in the ship and he was not going to show fear. He forced his mind into its usual orderly way of thought, only incidentally observing—like a footnote to a thesis—the physiological symptoms of tension manifesting themselves as he found his shoes and his life jacket. Then he made his way up the sloping deck to the door on the heels of the purser, and out into the windy darkness toward his station for "abandon ship".

For many years after the torpedoing of the *Wilhelmina* he was able to recall clear-cut details of the abandoning of the ship; his mind, trained to observation, noted these details of a strange and new experience and stored them away. He learned about discipline. There were voices in the darkness; there was the tone of bravado in which unseen soldiers cracked jokes about their desperate situation, and there was the note of hysteria in other voices, and the stillness that ensued when the voice of one of the artillery lieutenants—cracking a little with strain and yet under control—ordered silence.

"Don't act like kids," added the lieutenant. "You're men." Blanke at thirty-one felt, even at that moment,

72

an odd twinge at hearing someone of twenty-four speaking like that to soldiers of twenty.

The voice of the Dutch third mate, stumbling over his English, could now be heard.

"All right, thank you," said the lieutenant, and then to the soldiers, "Get into the boat."

Several flashlights made a pool of light in the darkness, and out of the pool the men climbed in, hastily but with hardly a sign of panic, although another rasping order from the lieutenant was necessary to impose silence again as the crowding began. Blanke stood waiting his turn beside the Army officers. He felt someone plucking at his sleeve. Someone—the second mate, he thought, but he could not be sure in the darkness—thrust a piece of paper into his hand.

"Position and course," said the man and then hastened off again toward the next boat before Blanke could reply. He put the paper into his pocket, ready to hand it over to whoever would be in command of the boat, and then there was a ridiculous moment of politeness as to whether he should climb in before or after the lieutenant. Then they sprang in together, pushing in among the soldiers, and after them came two of the Javanese deck hands, silent as always and insinuating themselves between the close-packed bodies on the thwarts.

There were Dutch orders shouted from the deck, and a clanking of machinery. The boat lurched and swung hideously in the darkness, crashed against the ship's side, swung and hit the invisible water with a splash amid yells from the soldiers, and then came soaring up on a black invisible wave and rolled horribly, as if she were going to turn over, righted herself

73

at what seemed the last possible second, and then sank down again more unpleasantly than any elevator Blanke had ever experienced. Not until much later did he come to realise how fortunate they were to have reached the water at all without capsizing; the Javanese deck hands had done a neat piece of work at bow and stern.

It was the blackest overcast night anyone could imagine; the *Wilhelmina* was already out of sight, the more so as the soldiers who had flashlights in the boat were using them freely—one shone straight into Blanke's face and left him quite blinded.

"What do we do next, sir?" asked the artillery lieutenant beside him.

"I can't see a thing," was all Blanke could say at the moment.

The lieutenant lifted his voice in a bellow as he ordered the flashlights extinguished. "Save 'em until you need 'em," he said.

The boat lurched and rolled again, soaring up and then dropping down, the abrupt descent marked by wails from the soldiers. The Pacific swell which the *Wilhelmina* hardly noticed had free play on the small boat; moreover, the brisk trade wind was turning her round slowly in a series of circles, so that each successive swell met her at a different angle, and her rolling and lurching were unpredictable in the darkness.

"Parm me," said the lieutenant, with a blurry attempt at politeness, and then he was horribly seasick—so, judging from the sounds, were most of the soldiers. So was Blanke, after struggling with his symptoms for several minutes. He had never known such misery as overcame him then. The world was

74

utterly pitiless, and he was hopeless and useless, and death would be welcome when it came, especially when the boat rolled wildly again, from far over to one side to far over to the other; a good deal of water slapped in, calling forth startled cries from the men it wetted.

Luckily for everyone concerned, that scientific mind of Blanke's continued to function. It could not help analysing the reasons for that uncontrolled and un-predictable motion of the boat. It was unpredictable simply because it was uncontrolled. The boat was spinning, slowly but helplessly, under the influence of the wind and should be brought under control so as to meet the rollers end on. Blanke's mind went back into the high-school physics and mechanics he had studied fourteen years before, picked out the relevant facts and proceeded to build up suggestions upon them. If something could be put up to catch the wind at the tail end—at the stern—the boat would turn like a weathercock and point into the wind and, pre-sumably, into the waves. That would be a good idea, but he did not see how it could be done in the dark. Similarly, if something could drag in the sea at the other end—at the bow—the boat would trail back from it, with bows to wind and sea. That might work very well if it could be done, but Blanke was not too sure how to set about it; it was the crowding and the darkness, in other words, which prevented Blanke from re-inventing the sea anchor that night.

The rudder, of course, would only function if the boat had some motion of its own through the water. Of course! The boat had an engine. If that were set running, someone could hold the rudder and steer her so as to meet the waves properly. He remembered that while he was waiting his turn to get into the boat, he had heard one of the other boats, with an engine running, leaving the ship.

"Hadn't we better get the engine started?" he said to the artillery lieutenant and realised as he said it that the lieutenant was too far gone with seasickness to be rational.

Blanke would have to deal with it himself. With the need for instant action, he put aside the temptation to follow up a new line of thought regarding the effect of military discipline on the young men crowded into the boat; they were used to receiving orders and drilled into obeying them. No time for such thoughts now. Blanke got cautiously off his thwart and began to push his way in the direction in which one of the Javanese deck hands had disappeared when they got in the boat. He had to climb over shoulders; he trod on bodies lying in the bottom, bodies that hardly resented the pressure of his foot.

"Where's that sailor?" he demanded. "Where's that Javanese?"

"Here, sir—back here," croaked a voice.

Blanke shook the Javanese's shoulder. "Motor. Engine," he said.

The Javanese said something in reply. Blanke felt his wrist held and his hand guided; that was the tiller —he knew the word from the glossary in the *Bluejacket's Manual*—a short piece of iron or wood used to turn the rudder. It swung unresisting in his hand; of course, that would be the case if the boat had no motion through the water. The Javanese had left his side; Blanke had the impression that the seaman was climbing forward by the route he himself had followed, over the heads and shoulders of the crowded soldiers. He waited tensely; he heard the Javanese call out something to his compatriot, who answered. He heard noises and expostulations which indicated that soldiers were being heaved out of the way; he heard a clatter and clanking of metal—during this time the boat had pitched and rolled excruciatingly a dozen times, and three times water had slopped in over the sides.

There came a sudden roar of the engines, and Blanke felt the rudder come to life under his hand. The roar ceased; the rudder died, but then the engine roared again, confidently, with every promise of permanence, and the water over the stern boiled, and the rudder bit. They were frightening, those first few seconds; it took Blanke that long to grasp the technique of turning the tiller the opposite way— during those seconds the boat slithered precariously along a crest and came nearer to capsizing than ever before, amid cries of dismay from the passengers. But by the time the boat had completed the circle, Blanke had matters almost under control. He met the next wave bows on; there was infinite satisfaction at first in doing so, in feeling the boat climbing the slope, but when they reached the crest and put their bows down and their stern up, and shot down the farther side, it was not so comfortable—in fact, it felt hideously dangerous.

He wanted to saw at the rudder, but restrained himself with the thought that that would be more dangerous still, but then his doubts were resolved by a sudden drop in the pitch of the engine's roar. He could feel the speed moderate, and the boat breasted the next slope more satisfactorily still and pitched over the crest in a manner quite restrained, so that some sort of small cheer came from the passengers capable of any sensation at all. Blanke guessed that the Javanese at the engine had throttled down, and he was grateful, even though he had little attention to spare for them; he had to concentrate on the feel of the wind on his face, on the lurch of the boat and on reminding himself to pull the tiller to the left—to port—when he wanted to head to the right—to starboard.

In a few minutes it was becoming second nature to him. Seasickness was forgotten; there was actually something exhilarating in handling the boat like this as she chugged valiantly forward in the dark. Where he was going he did not know, but he reconciled himself to that by telling himself that until daylight should come and new arrangements could be made, he was doing the only safe thing. Thinking along that line, he realised why there was no ship's officer in the boat—this was the chief engineer's boat, and he could guess what had happened to the chief engineer. The instant helplessness of the *Wilhelmina* after the torpedo struck told of a hit in the engine room; the chief engineer had died for his country.

That gloomy train of thought was interrupted by his overhearing a fragment of conversation among the soldiers just in front of him.

"There's lockers under these seats. Let's have your flash a minute, Joe."

"Leave those lockers alone," snapped Blanke; strain and excitement put an edge on his voice.

In four years of research he had had painful experience with over-enthusiastic, or stupid, or inquisitive laboratory assistants, and he could guess at what disasters might ensue if prying fingers got to work on those lockers. But he was astonished at the intensity of his speech—he would never have snapped at technical assistants in that way, but then his life was not in danger.

The fact was that the steadying of the boat's motion and the comforting thought circulating among the soldiers that the Navy was now in charge, were encouraging the more active of the young soldiers to indulge their innate restlessness.

"Move over, can't you?" said a voice.

"Get off my feet, you big slob," said another.

"Wish I had a drink," said a third.

It seemed as if in no time at all the unseen passengers were beginning to surge about in the boat; Blanke, keyed up to the highest pitch, was acutely conscious of variation in the trim, even if he did not use that word to himself. He only knew that it felt dangerous when the boat went down on one side and that it was likely to interfere with his steering. He opened his mouth to expostulate—and then shut it again while he rehearsed what he was going to say. He had to give an order; he had to shout into the wind, so that he would have to use all his lung power. He took a deep breath, told himself that he must display no agitation and then let himself go.

"Sit still, all of you!" he yelled.

It was gratifying that he made so much noise, and the result was gratifying, too, in that there was quiet in the boat and that someone, presumably the lieutenant, endorsed his order.

"Sergeant, see that the men keep still over there."

"Yes, sir."

There was much to be said for discipline when it produced such results. But, on the other hand, the cessation of the bustling in the boat and his growing familiarity with the handling of the tiller gave Blanke an opportunity to think again. He began to wonder what would happen next, and what he ought to do— if anything. He was the biggest fraud who had ever held a tiller. When daylight came, decisions would have to be reached. They would have to set that course which was written on the paper in his pocket. "They"—whom did he mean by "they"? The Javanese? The artillery lieutenant? He had an uneasy feeling that by "they" he really meant himself.

There must be a compass in the boat—otherwise there was no reason for the paper with the course written on it. He presumed he could set a course. He had no idea where he was—the word had gone round the ship that they were four days from Nouméa, and four days would mean what? A thousand miles, fifteen hundred miles? There certainly would not be gasoline to last all that time. They would have to use the sails—he had seen masts in the boat and presumed that there were sails. He found himself hoping devoutly that the Javanese deck hands knew something about sailing a boat. There was a chance that daylight would reveal one or more of the other boats near them, but Blanke could guess how small a chance that was; he could work out in his mind how limited was the horizon from a small boat and how widely dispersed the boats could become during several hours with a brisk wind blowing.

As he reached that conclusion it became borne in upon him that he could now see something of the boat and its crowded passengers; he could see the heads and shoulders in front of him as dark masses in a lighter medium. Daylight was actually coming, and he stirred in his seat to discover he was horribly stiff, and his hand ached from its vice-like grip on the tiller, and he was shivering with cold.

"Well, there it is, boys," said a voice in the boat, and everyone started chattering at once—at least everyone who was not too cold or seasick to chatter. The light increased rapidly, and he could see the unshaven cheeks and the drawn features of the packed crowd. He could see the two Javanese crouching by the engine, and the young lieutenant perched on a thwart near them. The lieutenant rose with infinite stiffness and pushed his way to the stern of the boat and into a minute space beside Blanke.

"What do we do now, sir?" he asked, speaking in a muffled tone in an effort not to be overheard by the soldiers crowded all round.

The question, and the manner of asking it, confirmed Blanke in his certainty that the artillery lieutenant, although perfectly qualified to command an anti-aircraft platoon, had not the least idea what to do when adrift in the Pacific with fifty castaways.

"Let's look round," said Blanke, temporising.

The lieutenant agreed without making any move to follow up the suggestion, and Blanke knew he had to act. He caught the eye of one of the Javanese by the engine and beckoned to him. Then he handed over the tiller and prepared to stand up. It was not going to be easy.

"Prop me up," he said, coming erect on his aching legs and preparing to mount on the thwart. Half a dozen hands were raised to hold him as he stood, wobbling dangerously in the heaving boat. There was nothing to see; he shifted his feet precariously as he turned to sweep the horizon. There was only the sea, only the long rollers marching toward them. The motion of the boat became more pronounced, and Blanke saw that half, or more than half, of the soldiers, carried away by his example, were scrambling to their feet to look around too; he ought to have expected that. He nearly missed his footing and exclaimed loudly, and the lieutenant had the sense to appreciate the danger.

"Sit down, you men. Sit down, all of you!"

He was obeyed, and Blanke stepped down and reseated himself.

"Nothing in sight," he said, and now he had to think quickly—rather, he did not have to think, but had to implement the decisions which the meditations of the night had forced upon him. He took the scrap of paper from his pocket and studied what was written on it: "Course 222° True. Var 11°E." He could interpret that, all right, thanks to the *Bluejacket's Manual*.

"I have the course here," he said. "I think we'll have to get under sail."

He was painfully conscious that fifty pairs of eyes had him under their scrutiny and that fifty lives might depend on his decisions. The Javanese beside him had caught the last word he said.

"Sail," said the Javanese and then pointed toward the engine. "Motor—stop."

The Javanese backed up his words with an eloquent gesture; he was clearly implying what Blanke had already thought of—that gas was likely to run short any moment.

"You see we'll have to—" said Blanke to the lieutenant; he was having to struggle against a curious constriction of the throat as he spoke. Then to the Javanese, "All right. Sail."

The Javanese nodded—he even smiled. He returned the tiller to Blanke, stood up and shouted in his own language to his fellow seaman. The two of them became immediately active, and Blanke was relieved to see that their movements were entirely purposeful and that they did not have to refer to him. They scrambled up and down the length of the boat, pushing the soldiers out of their way when necessary; the soldiers watched their actions with dull interest. There was a good deal of upheaval while the Javanese moved the soldiers off the lockers along the sides of the boat and dragged out grimy rolls of canvas and then busied themselves with the lines that came with them. There were two masts laid lengthways in the boat, and the Javanese raised first one and then the other—Blanke noted that they lay in opposite directions, sensibly, so as to call for the least movement to set them up. Each mast in turn had its base passed down through holes in the thwarts, and was settled down with comforting solidity into what Blanke knew—thanks to his scholar's memory—were called the "steps" below. The wire ropes attached to the tops of the masts were led out to the sides of the boat and hooked on to these; Blanke dived into his memory again to come up with the word "stays". Things were really moving too fast for his mental comfort. Already the Javanese were looking to him for orders, ready to set the sails. There must be a compass somewhere in the boat, otherwise he would not have been given that scrap of paper. Then before him he saw a small varnished trap door, which he raised in desperation, and underneath it was a compass. There were the words U.S. NAVY. BUSHIPS. No. 1 COMPASS, engraved on the ring—these lifeboats, of course, had been supplied by the Navy when the *Wilhelmina* had been chartered.

"I was wondering about a compass," said the artillery lieutenant, and Blanke forebore to say, "Not as much as I was." Instead he devoted himself, gratefully, to the deviation card inside the lid.

He plunged down into his memory again and, like the diver in the old ballad, came to the surface again with a pearl, "Can Dead Men Vote Twice?": Compass, Deviation, Magnetic, Variation, True—that was what the initial letters of those words stood for; the *Bluejacket's Manual* had told him so. He could perhaps have worked out the compass course from first principles, but the mnemonic saved time and trouble, besides reminding him forcibly of the need for correction. A few seconds' study of the deviation card revealed the huge importance of it, for it was a cumulative and not a self-cancelling correction. He had to subtract no less than 27 from 222.

With the pencil he had taken from his pocket he wrote down the resultant figure 195, on his scrap of paper, and then checked through his working again, swallowing hard with excitement as he did so. An uncorrected error of twenty-seven degrees in the course could mean a difference of dozens of miles in their destination, the difference perhaps between life and a lingering death out in the wastes of the Pacific. It was almost inconceivable that a man should be facing that grim possibility when less than three weeks earlier his chief doubt had been whether he would be awarded a Ph.D.

Now everybody was waiting for him again. Now he had to reach fresh decisions. He pinned his faith on the Javanese and beckoned to one of them and then gestured toward the tiller; to his relief he received a nod in return. They switched off the engine, and the man he had beckoned to came scrambling aft, where they made room for him at the tiller. Blanke showed his written 195 and pointed to the compass, and was reassured again by a nod. The Javanese understood and shouted in his own language to his compatriot and was answered in a rapid-fire conversation.

It was a moment of tense excitement—now that the engine had ceased running, the boat was beginning to wallow aimlessly again over the rollers. The other Javanese was pushing his way through the crowd and putting ropes in the men's hands; and then with gestures he called on them to pull.

"Heave ho!" shouted someone, apparently thinking that was amusing.

With a creaking and groaning the sails began to rise up the masts. There was a moment of chaos, a moment when Blanke felt consuming doubt which later he realised was fear. The sails flapped with a thunderous din, and the boat lurched and pitched horribly. The Javanese at the sails was leaping about the boat, over heads and shoulders, attending to this and that. The boat lay over momentarily worse than ever, and then the Javanese at the tiller pulled it far over and she steadied herself. The sea bubbled round the rudder, and, inconceivably, order emerged from the chaos. The Javanese at the sails was still leaping about, pulling at ropes, but obviously he was only making minor adjustments.

Blanke looked at the compass, and there was the lubber's line swinging close about 195 degrees. He looked up at the sails, and they were bellying out, but under restraint, and the Javanese attending to them was hauling them in to a slightly closer angle, with the help of soldiers, into whose hands he was putting the ropes. He was pushing and gesticulating at some of the men to induce them to move across the boat and sit on the other side—that made an appreciable difference to the feeling of stability. For the boat was lying over, with the wind coming sideways at them; Blanke's mind promptly grappled with the deduction that on a course of 222 degrees True, in an area where the southeast trades prevailed, the wind would naturally come in over the side; he looked up at the sails again and down at the boat and thought about the triangle of forces at work which would drive the boat in a direction different from that of the wind.

And it was surprising, too, to see how differently the boat was behaving. Even though she was not heading directly into the waves, she was not lurching so wildly nor so menacingly as she did when not under control. Her behaviour was actually purposeful;

86

under the steadying influence of the sails, she was yielding to the rollers in a measured fashion, with a rise and a roll and a pitch that actually had some aesthetic quality about it. The water—the "wake", that was the word—bubbled behind him; a few fragments of spray were flying from the bows. Blanke was astonished at the discovery that this might almost be thought of as pleasant; and when, some moments later, the clouds parted sufficiently to allow the rising sun to shine on his back, he contrasted his previous feeling of despairing misery with what might almost be described now as well-being. He caught the eye of the Javanese at the tiller; busy though this man might be, darting vigilant glances up at the sails and down at the compass and over the side at the rollers, he yet could find a moment to grin at him in a sort of conspiratorial confidence.

There was a perceptible change in the soldiers too. Except for two unfortunates who were still far gone in seasickness, they were all talking at once. Cigarettes were being smoked in such numbers that the wind was carrying off a small trail of smoke—to "leeward", that was the word. And already there were cries of despair as cigarettes were counted up; there were men with none and men with a few and none with many. Every soldier in the boat was cursing the suddenness of the alarm which had set them adrift without a chance of gathering up precious possessions. Then, almost immediately, there were remarks made loudly by one and another, and questions asked of the sergeants, obviously intended to reach the lieutenant's ears. The soldiers were hungry and thirsty and they wanted to eat and drink.

The lieutenant turned to Blanke. "Any orders, sir?"

Blanke could not answer immediately. The difference in the size of his collar insignia—smaller than that of the Army—marked him as the only Navy officer in the boat. But that no more qualified him for the command than did his greater age. If by chance there had been present the lowliest, most newly joined seaman second class, that seaman would legally be in command. The oak leaf and acorn on Blanke's collar specifically disqualified him; the *Bluejacket's Manual* was quite definite about that. Yet, despite all this, Blanke could not close his mental eyes to the obvious fact that the course of previous events had conferred the command on him. And reluctantly he faced the next fact, which was that if he were to disclaim all responsibility and throw in his hand, the result might easily be disastrous for all on board. There were many long difficult days ahead, and the occupants of the boat had come to look on him as possessed of all the technical knowledge necessary. That confidence, baseless though it might be, was an asset of supreme importance. He could not evade the trust reposed in him; yet he still longed to temporise.

The boat corkscrewed over a roller, and the water that had entered the boat surged over the bottom boards and slapped against his ankles—it had done that a hundred times already and had ceased to attract his notice until now, when he was looking for an excuse to evade decision. He seized on the chance; and that brought to his notice what the bottom of the boat was like, after that horrible night.

"Don't you think the first thing to do," he said mildly, "is to clean up? Look at all this."

The lieutenant might be a man who feared responsibility, but he was open to suggestion. "Quite right, sir," he said and then he lifted up his voice. "At ease!"

It was interesting how the commotion died away—interesting to notice the easy manner of the lieutenant, accustomed to command and expecting to be obeyed.

"We're going to get the boat cleaned up," the lieutenant went on. "Sergeant Schwartz, I want everyone at work."

Discipline, not too deeply rooted among those young soldiers, had a hard struggle against the complete novelty of the situation. The buzz of talk reasserted itself, but the lieutenant was ready for that.

"No breakfast until the boat's policed," he said. "Sergeant Schwartz, you heard my order."

So now, while the soldiers were at work bailing out and clearing up, the lieutenant turned to Blanke to discuss the next problem, which he had already raised by his last speech.

"What do we do about that, sir?" he asked. "What about food and water?"

Blanke was already turning over in his mind what the *Bluejacket's Manual* had to say about Survival Afloat and he supplemented that with what he had learned during his medical training. He opened the locker beside him and saw with relief that it was filled with small cans—he really had not doubted that it would be, but he was relieved, all the same.

"How long before we're rescued, sir?" asked the lieutenant.

Blanke felt acute irritation. He wanted to turn upon the lieutenant and point out that he did not know where he was, had only a vague idea of where he was going and could form no estimate of the speed between these points. The violence of his feelings surprised him; it was really shocking to find that there was something alluring about the prospect of losing his temper and flaring out, uncontrolled, in a wild outburst to compensate himself for the things life was doing to him and for the responsibilities piling on him.

The realisation steadied him; it was the more easy to maintain his self-control because he was interested in the discovery that he was liable to such fits of rage even though he could not remember ever having had one before. Lastly, he remembered the *Bluejacket's Manual* again. There were a few lines there about the initial feeling of "relief and elation" when finding oneself in a lifecraft away from the sinking wreck, followed by a warning that these attitudes might "worsen into irritability and preoccupation". That book was certainly accurate. He almost smiled at the thought and, in consequence, could make himself talk with studied calm. He posed as if he had been accustomed all his life to dealing with problems of death and survival.

"We'll have to go carefully right from the start," he said heavily and unemotionally.

"Of course, sir."

"Each of these cans is a day's ration for one man. We'll have to halve that. Two meals a day—one can between four men at each meal."

"Yes, sir."

Blanke looked round again; his mind recovered another word from the glossary—those small barrels were called "breakers," but whatever their name, there were not too many of them.

"Of course, water's more important still," he said, in the same emotionless voice. "One pint a day—a quarter of a pint four times a day."

"Yes, sir. We'll start as we mean to go on," said the lieutenant helpfully.

That was indeed how they went on. By the second meal all novelty had worn off, and the healthy twenty-year-old appetites of the soldiers were insulted at the attempt to satisfy them with four sugar tablets and two malt tablets and one stick of chewing gum. A quarter of a pint of water went in two gulps, almost unnoticed. There were signs of that depression and reaction which the *Manual* warned against. The sun, which had so gratefully warmed them at dawn, turned into an enemy, fierce and unrelenting.

It was lucky for everyone in the boat that Blanke's orderly and active mind—the mind of a trained observer, seeking always a vent for its activity—was in charge. He noted at once that it would be impossible for the two Javanese to attend all the time to the tiller and the sails; moreover—grim thought—one of them might die. It was necessary to train replacements, so every half hour a fresh man came back to the tiller and studied how, under the grinning tuition of the Javanese (those Javanese stayed miraculously cheerful and were always ready with a polite grin as a substitute for words), to keep the boat steady on her course and to stand by what Blanke doubtfully called the "sheets"—he could not be quite sure of his memory regarding that word.

There was the horrible cramped discomfort of sitting up in the boat. Blanke realised that it was hardly necessary for the life jackets still to be worn. Removing them added considerably to the available room, and, as well, the life jackets could be used as a mattress in the one available space in the middle of the boat, whereon nine men at a time—nine out of fifty-four—could indulge themselves in the unspeakable luxury of stretching out straight and going to sleep.

Three hours of sleeping stretched out was very comforting and refreshing. Blanke chose that interval because then the cycle shifted through the day and gave everyone an equal chance of sleeping in the dark or in the daylight.

Naturally it was not very long before the survivors wanted to know how long the voyage would last, and Blanke, warned by his experience with the lieutenant, managed to decide upon an answer.

"Let's say a thousand miles," he said. "It may be more, but let's say that to start with."

At once everyone wanted to know at what speed they were travelling. No one could be sure, and even in the steady trade winds their speed was obviously variable. It took Blanke half a day to come up with the solution. Probably it was not an original reinvention of the old-fashioned ship's log; more likely some scrap of schoolboy reading had survived in Blanke's memory. At any rate, he took one of the long lines in the boat, knotted it at six-foot lengths (Sergeant Schwartz was just six-feet tall, he said), attached a couple of empty ration cans to the end and let it run out astern while timing it against the second hand of his watch.

So that was another item in the routine, one in which everyone was interested. Every half hour the log was cast, and the calculation made while everyone waited breathlessly. There were groans of despair when the speed was announced as being only 2.1 miles an hour; there was elation when it was 3.9—and another figure added to the column Blanke kept on the back of the deviation card, mounting up toward the arbitrary thousand that Blanke had selected, and only Blanke gave a thought to the fact that each result might easily be 50 per cent in error.

There were other breaks in the day. Early in the first afternoon one of the Javanese rose hastily from where he was sitting, like a statue, in the middle of the boat, and called the attention of his colleague to something on the horizon. At the sight of what they saw, one of them came hastily back to the tiller while the other went to tend the sails. Blanke saw the squall approaching; he had seen similar ones from the deck of the *Wilhelmina* and had observed them with interest; but if it had not been for the Javanese, he would not have attached the importance to it demanded by an overcrowded small boat.

They dropped the big sail in the middle, which surely must be the mainsail, and they reduced the little triangular sail in front, leaving undisturbed the little rectangular sail on the mast in the stern. By that time, the squall was close upon them. When the boat rose on a wave, Blanke could see a grey line on the surface of the water, straight as if drawn with a ruler, advancing close upon them. Even before it reached

93

them, preliminary gusts of wind roared at them, laying the boat over amid cries of alarm from the soldiers until the Javanese pulled the tiller over, turning the boat into the wind, and then she rode more steadily, while the wind howled about them, and the spray flew in sheets, and finally the rain came deluging down. The sail at the stern produced the weathercock effect that Blanke had already thought of. He ran through the glossary in his mind; what they had done was to "heave to"—an expression with an odd old-time flavour. Yet, with that wind howling and the sea screaming around them, to heave to meant to live; not to do so meant to die. He noted the rigidity with which he was sitting, the intensity with which he felt the greater gusts, his quickened heart-beat and the dryness of his mouth. This was fear again, intense physical fear.

There was a man over there—there was another—as frightened as he was, or even more. Fear could grip sturdy boys who had not completed high school just as much as it could Ph.D.'s. One of them was looking at him with staring eyes as if appealing to him, looking to him for safety or reassurance. Blanke made a huge effort. He told his muscles to relax, he forced his limbs into an easier attitude, he made himself turn toward the Javanese at the tiller with a nod and a smile which he hoped did not appear like the death's head grin he felt it to be. Then he glanced back at the scared soldier with every appearance of casual confidence he could manage. It seemed to help, even though at that moment the squall burst into its final paroxysm, changing direction several times, slightly but sufficiently to lay the boat over, horrifyingly, before she swung to it. Then a final roaring Niagara of rain, and the squall was over. On the far side of it the sun shone, and the sea was blue again, with the great rollers marching mechanically and predictably toward them.

"Say, cap'n," said a voice. "Cap'n."

Blanke realised with an effort that it was he who was being addressed by this title. "Yes?"

"That rain's salt. I've been trying to drink it."

Blanke tried to explain that with the spray flying, any rain would be tainted with sea water. He devoted thought to the question of devising a means to collect pure rain water during a squall, but in all that voyage he never succeeded. It never rained, as it happened, without wind and spray.

But the squall called more forcibly to his attention the problem of "leeway"—so he called it, self-consciously, to himself. The boat would move sideways to some extent with the wind over the side, and when they were hove to, she would drift considerably stern first before the wind. Allowance must be made for that. Blanke drew mental pictures of the triangle of forces at work on the boat, and arbitrarily selected ten degrees as a suitable correction. His announcement of the revised course was received without comment. The new course brought them closer to the wind, and that accentuated the odd aesthetic pleasure of thrashing along with the spray flying from the "weather bow". It was stimulating even to the most fainthearted and depressed of the passengers.

So depression and despair were combated during that voyage. There was the half-hourly relieving of the tiller and sheets, and the half-hourly heaving of the log, the three-hourly change-over on the life-jacket mattress and the occasional hasty heaving to when squalls approached. They had to heave to each evening as soon as it was too dark to have adequate warning of squalls. Sergeant Schwartz came up surprisingly with a remarkable plan during the dark evenings, for he started a spelling bee. Only a few men agreed to play, but the competition soon grew keen, and the onlookers were interested in spite of themselves. It was inevitable and highly significant that Blanke should be called upon as arbitrator over disputed points of spelling. There were language classes—in other words, attempts to teach English to the two Javanese, while the soldiers listened with amused interest to the polite efforts of the Javanese to explain to them the intricacies of their own language and of Dutch.

Any distraction was better than crouching idle in the boat, waiting for the moment when two sips of water per man was to be rationed out, waiting for four sugar tablets and two malted-milk tablets. Anything was better than to sit in black despair, in melancholy moodiness that might change at any moment into a flare-up of murderous rage. The pettiest, most trivial, most infantile distractions were of help.

Blanke came to learn quickly enough that the fifty young soldiers in the boat were fifty individuals, and not an undifferentiated mass of bristly faces. He came to know all of them, and in the long dark nights he came to know all the hoarse croaking voices, too, one distinct from another. Within a short time he knew the cheerful and the helpful, and the surly and the depressed.

Besides hunger and thirst, there was hideous physical discomfort, sitting eternally—with one blessed interval of stretching out on the mattress every eighteen hours—on unyielding seats. Damp salt on the skin and in the clothes as the spray dried made a man feel as if he would willingly tear off his skin. By the fourth day boils began to appear; nearly every man on board suffered from them. The sixth evening was marked by the presence of enough moon to make it possible to keep sail set for an hour and more after sunset and add a few more daily miles toward the absurd goal of a thousand miles which Blanke had set, and each successive night the period lengthened.

On the thirteenth day at noon they were still heading on their course. The sun was almost exactly overhead, blazing down upon them, the boat was maintaining its monotonous rise and fall, heel and pitch, with all the crowded heads and bodies swaying in unison as it did so. Then Private First Class Sanderson in the bow raised his head.

"Listen, you guys!"

They listened.

"What d'you think you can hear—harps?" croaked a voice.

"Listen!" repeated Sanderson.

Then another man heard it, and another.

"That's a plane!"

Everyone began to scramble to his feet, even the men on the mattress.

"Sit down! Sit down!" shrieked Blanke, his dry throat seeming to split with the effort.

It was one of the most dangerous moments of the voyage; it called for the united influence of the more levelheaded to restrain the excitement and to make the men sit down, fifty heads turning, fifty pairs of eyes searching the sky.

"There it is!"

The little speck was visible to them all.

"Maybe it's a Jap," said Marx the pessimist, but that suggestion could not prevail long with an anti-aircraft unit trained in plane identification.

"It's a Kingfisher!"

"Is he going to see us?"

They watched with terrible intensity; some men were uttering prayers, and others blasphemy.

At 2,000 feet the plane was heading a little away from them. Then the plane altered course.

"He's seen us!"

They tried to cheer; they started to stand up again.

"Sit down!" shrieked Blanke again—he had a memory of one piece of research wasted and ruined and necessitating restarting, all because of excited haste in the final technique. But if the boat overturned, there would be no restarting.

Straight for them came the plane. It dived and skimmed close above them, then wagged its wings and circled and made it obvious that they had been seen; it was also obvious that the plane would be unable to land on the rough water. Then it turned and headed back the way it had come; the prayers that followed it were prayers of thankfulness now, and the blasphemies were expressions of joy. Then every eye turned upon Blanke, the man who knew everything, to learn how soon they would be rescued.

"Not until tomorrow," said Blanke, doing hasty mental calculations based on the most fragile of data.

"Not until tomorrow evening at the very earliest. But we can all have an extra ration of water this minute."

Seeing how utterly ignorant he was regarding the radius of action of a Kingfisher, and what shipping there might be at whatever base the plane had flown from, if it had flown from a land base, the guess was reasonably accurate—it was exactly twenty-four hours before the mine sweeper showed up on the horizon, and twenty-five hours before they were being helped up on to her deck, nearly twenty-six hours before Blanke was cautiously sipping at the cup of coffee which had haunted his unspoken thoughts for fourteen days.

"Boon?" said the mine sweeper's captain when Blanke gave the name of his ship in answer to the captain's question. "She's in at Tongatabu this minute—came in as escort to a torpedoed cruiser. You'll be able to join her at once."

Blanke was still too utterly weary to mention the fact that he had believed all this time that he was steering for Nouméa and had never heard of Tongatabu in his life until now. But he had sailed the lifeboat 400 miles straight toward Tongatabu all the same, 400 miles that made the difference between life and death.

So it was at Tongatabu that Blanke first set foot on the deck of a destroyer. It was there that he reported to the officer of the deck in the words he had rehearsed repeatedly after the mine sweeper's captain had taught them to him.

"Lieutenant Malcolm Blanke reporting aboard for duty, sir. I regret to report I have lost my orders while en route, sir."

The officer of the deck smiled politely and—to his credit—not the least broadly.

"We've been expecting you, doctor. But not in this condition. No baggage, I take it? Then I'll take you to the skipper right away."

The Kingfisher had spread the news of the sighted lifeboat the day before, and Commander Angell, captain of the *Boon*, did not need explanations of Blanke's presence. He made Blanke cordially welcome. Then he went on to say, "I'm certainly glad you've arrived, doctor. We've a plague of cockroaches on board, and I expect you to turn to right away to get rid of them."

Counterpunch

It was one more moment in history when the *Boon* approached the Golden Gate, returning to the American continent after a year in the Pacific—ten months of peace and two of war, ten months of gradually accelerating movement and two months of torrential happenings. The river of American history had flowed faster and faster, and yet its leap over the precipice that was Pearl Harbor had been a surprise. Now the river was pouring tumultuously down the cataract below the falls, bursting in spray amid rocks and whirlpools.

It was evening here in the Pacific; across the continent it was already deep night. Very possibly over in the Atlantic, at the moment when the *Boon* swung to enter the Golden Gate, a torpedo was leaving its tube, and another flaming wreck was lighting the Atlantic seaboard where a bold enemy was ravaging American waters, sinking American ships, taking American lives and draining away the American lifeblood.

An insane mêlée was raging over the entire world. Two months ago the American giant had been dealt a stunning and unexpected blow and now, assailed on every side, the giant was struggling to keep on his feet and regain his strength so that he could strike down his enemies.

On board the American destroyer U.S.S. *Boon*, hovering outside the Golden Gate, there was little enough thought devoted to the fact that this was history. They were home again after a year of duty. Officers and enlisted men could barely contain their impatience while the *Boon* circled in the darkening haze, keeping guard to seaward as the three transports she had escorted from Honolulu made their dilatory way in through the novel harbour defences across the twilit yet still invisible Gate.

Cmdr. Edward Angell, striding impatiently out to the wing of the bridge, saw the light wink a fresh message from the shore and listened as the signalman read it to him.

"Acknowledge," he said over one shoulder—and then, over the other, he gave the orders that would bring the *Boon* into the bay, "Course zero nine four. All engines ahead standard."

They came nosing their way in through the thin rain. The transports were already safely berthed; the net defences were already closing behind the destroyer and Angell had just given the order which would take the *Boon* in to her pier when another winking light called forth a fresh order from Angell and swung the ship round again. They would not see any more of San Francisco that evening than that watery glance had already revealed to them, for the new signal curtly ordered, "Proceed Mare Island Navy Yard immediately for interim docking. Arrival conference scheduled 2000."

The word that they were not calling in San Francisco went round the ship like lightning, and the *Boon* left an invisible wake of curses behind her as she turned her stern to the city and groped her way through the chill rain of the night up the bay to Mare Island.

Friedmann, the executive officer, acting in his other capacity as navigator on the darkened bridge, peered down at the chart and slid his rulers across it to ascertain the course, first to The Brothers and then round San Pablo Point and then along the buoyed channel to where the lights of Mare Island awaited them. Angell was content to leave the business to him; the final words of the signal occupied his own mind.

It was a little startling that an arrival conference would be held at twenty hundred—within a few minutes of reaching Mare Island. It certainly seemed that the Navy was taking the war seriously. Angell ran in his mind through his "job-order box," in which was listed all the work that should be done on his ship, in order of priority and also in order of ease of performance. That would be his contribution to this eight-o'clock conference. And over there Richmond was ablaze with lights—those were the new shipyards, now working three shifts to turn out merchant shipping, building the red corpuscles of the lifeblood of the free nations. The last time Angell had visited San Francisco Bay the lights had been a little farther south, where a host of men were working round the clock to complete the stands and clubhouses for a new race track—labor and materials being consumed with American prodigality even when the national danger crept nearer and nearer.

Angell shook off the memory to devote his thoughts to the present situation, to his ship and to the men who manned her. No doubt everyone on board knew of the signal which had sent them to Mare Island, but the ship's company must be informed officially in a manner which would assure them that their captain was aware of their disappointment and was not merely callous or despairing. Angell growled an order, and within seconds the public-address system through the ship came alive.

"Now hear this. Now hear this."

After that introduction Angell spoke into the instrument himself. The bad temper which had put an edge to his voice evaporated as he did so. He was as one with his ship's company in his disappointment, and they knew it; but the Navy was a solid entity—from the Chief of Naval Operations down to the latest recruit—and the men he was addressing knew that too.

There were wives and children in San Francisco; there were women and girl friends; there were liquor, music, entertainment; there was the inexpressibly keen pleasure of temporary freedom from plans of the day and supervision and enforced crowding in with others. But the *Boon* was under orders for Mare Island. And here they were, nearing the breakwater, and the civilian pilot was coming on board to lay them alongside the finger pier, bright in the blazing lights which revealed all the feverish activity of the yard.

The lines were hardly secured before a dozen men were ready to come on board—naval officers and civilians in approximately equal numbers.

"Planners and estimators," was their brief explanation of themselves to Coleman, the officer of the deck.

Angell led them to the little wardroom, which they filled. One single glance exchanged between Angell and the wardroom steward, without a word being spoken, postponed dinner once more, this time to an indefinite future.

"Sorry to rush you like this, cap'n," said the commander who had led the party. "But we want to have our workmen on board here tomorrow morning at oh-eight-hundred."

"Get all the sleep you can tonight," said a tall thin civilian with a briefcase. "Three shifts from then on, chipping and hammering."

"Your yard period ends at midnight on the fifth," the commander went on. "You're due to take a convoy the morning of the sixth."

"Very well," said Angell; there was nothing else to say. That standard answer was probably evolved to meet situations just like this.

In reply, the briefcases were opened all round the table in one simultaneous movement, as if at drill; but the entrance of two more officers at the wardroom door minimised the effect.

"Pardon me a moment, gentlemen," said Angell. "This is my executive officer, Lieutenant Commander Friedmann."

Angell's first glance had revealed no more to him than that the other new arrival was not one of the ship's officers. His second glance now surprised him— this was his young cousin and old shipmate, George. He rose instinctively to his feet even while he told

105

himself that this was no time for family calls. Friedmann forestalled anything he had to say.

"I'm being relieved, sir," he said. "My relief, Lieutenant Brown."

"Glad to have you on board, lieutenant," said Angell—there was a scrap of Navy jargon to meet every situation—and George, standing at attention, conformed to procedure. Angell turned back to Friedmann. "You're leaving us, Carl?"

"Yes, sir. I'm going to new construction—in command. Lieutenant Brown has informed me my orders are on the way."

"Congratulations. I'm delighted, of course," said Angell. "You deserve it."

Those were formal words, too, but perfectly genuine. Friedmann would make an excellent destroyer captain, as Angell had more than once stated in his fitness reports. But the formality was of assistance in enabling Angell to conceal his dismay at losing his executive officer at this crisis of his ship's career. Angell was aware that cousin George was a very competent officer, but he knew nothing of the ship and her condition and nothing of her personnel problems. For the next day or two it would mean a heavier load on his own shoulders.

"You had both better stay here and hear what these gentlemen have to say," he said, and his glance directed itself especially to cousin George. "You'll need to know what's in the wind."

"Aye aye, sir." Each of them uttered the three syllables exactly to time; nor did it occur to anyone present to moralise over the fact that a polite suggestion like "you had better", when uttered by a senior officer, was as forceful as any specific order.

The wardroom table, when they joined the group sitting round it, was now covered with plans of the ship, and no time was wasted in opening the conference.

"We're installing radar," said the commander. The tone of his voice implied that this was a most solemn moment, but the first impression on Angell's mind apparently did not quite correspond.

"Yes?" he said tentatively. The word was still new to him. Radar was something he had read about in confidential documents, something the British had used with effect on occasions—a piece of equipment that a battleship might carry with advantage. The United States Navy had been making tentative experiments with it. He had actually once seen a rotating bedspring at a ship's mast. It had hardly occurred to him that a destroyer might be equipped with one of these instruments. He knew that to a nation at war each one would be far mare valuable than the Koh-i-noor and he harbored suspicions that it might be temperamental. The next point that came up in his mind drew forth the question that every captain would be certain to ask.

"Where are you going to put it?" he said.

Captains of ships of war from the days of the Greek triremes had asked that question. A fighting vessel naturally was crammed with fighting equipment to make her the most effective fighting vessel her tonnage would allow. There could not be room for anything more. Angell's imagination was not nearly wild enough to envisage what the necessities of war to the death would eventually bring about in the matter of packing in additional weapons—and in the matter of hardship to the overcrowded men who would have the handling of them.

The commander was already indicating on the plan of the ship where the radar was to be inserted —not a simple operation, for the *Boon* was already a maze of pipes and wires and airducts which would have to be rerouted to make way for the intruder. Angell listened to the sweeping alterations proposed and then asked the next inevitable question.

"Who's going to maintain it?"

"We'll send you a trained radar man—nearly trained, anyway."

"One?"

"Yes. You'll have the manuals too, naturally."

Angell was already picturing the change of expression in the face of Klein, his communications officer, when he should be told that he would have the additional burden of responsibility for this instrument thrust upon his shoulders.

"Now, there are the K guns," went on the commander a little hastily. "You'll have two—aft, here and here."

"Won't they crowd the torpedo tubes?"

"There's just room for them. You'll be glad to have them when you're depth-charging a sub. With the K guns you can drop a pattern that will more than double your chance of a hit."

"So I understand," said Angell. He was not so clear as to how the K guns were going to be manned, nor how they would be fed with the necessary depth charges; but he could certainly foresee a drastic revision of the stations on the battle bill.

"I've four twenty-millimetre guns for you too," said the commander. "You need all the anti-aircraft protection you can carry."

"Thank you," said Angell. That meant more alterations to the battle bill. "Where d'you find room for the magazines?"

The commander had an answer to that question too, which he produced like a rabbit from a conjuror's hat. And when he had explained, he gave way to the civilian on his right, and the conference entered its next stage. In two hours the visitors' proposals were completed, and it was now Angell's turn to produce his Current Ship's Maintenance Project with its collection of cards, white and red and blue and yellow, and to state the needs of the ship as seen through the eyes of his heads of department—engineer officer and gunnery officer and first lieutenant. Up to now the conference had been trying to fit together a jigsaw puzzle in terms of space, fitting new appliances into the limited capacity of the *Boon*. Now it was a jigsaw puzzle in terms of time, trying to fit all the necessary operations into a schedule within the rigid frame of the eight days allowed—not so easy when some of them could not be begun until others were completed. Twice when the plans seemed complete, someone noticed an incompatibility, involving the presence of two different working teams on the same patch of deck at the same moment, and twice the weary process of reassembling the scheme had to be recommenced.

Then, the last paper was put away, and the last briefcase zipped closed, and the last visitor left the ship. Angell looked across the table through the wreaths of tobacco smoke at his executive officer and at cousin George as the three of them ate the sandwiches which came as a poor and late substitute for dinner.

"It looks to me," he said, "as if there'll be a man or two who can be spared—half a dozen, perhaps. Sort 'em out, and we'll give what leave we can. There are two cases of domestic hardship which need special consideration."

"Aye, aye, sir."

Angell glanced at the clock. "Those shore-duty types advised us to get in all the sleep possible tonight. Good night."

Angell was of the type that prefers to be awakened ten minutes earlier than necessary so as to make sure of sufficient time to drink the second cup of breakfast coffee at leisure. With regret he looked at his watch after a preliminary sip. The minutes were ticking away, and the leisure was about to end, as he knew only too well. It was going to be a complicated day. He finished his second cup and considered the possibility of a third. But that was as near as he came to it; for as he replaced his cup in the saucer, the first of his heads of department came in, papers in hand, with the first query regarding the programme of work. The day had begun. The ferries from Vallejo were crowded, and the next moment a wave of workmen came pouring on board the *Boon* to halt and face the flag as the public-address system of the yard played *The Star-Spangled Banner* and the colours soared up the masts.

It was halfway through the day when cousin George came hastily to him. "I've stopped the work on those K guns, sir," he said.

Angell switched his mind from the last problem to the new one. "Why?"

"Because of the torpedo tubes, sir. You asked last night about that. There's not enough clearance."

"I'll come and see," said Angell.

He made his way aft, through the fantastic bustle and din pervading every square yard of the ship, George at his heels. Between the torpedo tubes stood a group of idle welders; the work they had already begun marked the site of the new K gun. Angell squinted round, conjuring up a vision of the gun in position there. George was right. A K gun on each beam here would restrict the effective train of the tubes. The after tube could not fire forward, through a considerable arc, nor similarly would the forward tube fire aft. A K-gun enthusiast might well say that the loss was small, that a slight restriction on the employment of the torpedo tubes would be more than balanced by the ability to throw a wide pattern of depth charges. But that was fundamentally wrong; a destroyer existed to launch torpedoes, and not the least impairment of her power to do so could be tolerated.

"You're quite right, George," he said. "Get the planners over here at once. No more work's to be done here until this is settled."

"Here's my job order," said the leading welder.

"I don't care. No more work is to be done."

Eight days for the ship to be made ready and a card-castle schedule of work—the shifting of one

111

single item would imperil the whole programme. A convoy would be ready to be escorted to Pearl at the end of that eight days, and the Navy would be urgently awaiting it. It was not a wild possibility that the success or failure of a campaign might hinge on having *Boon* ready in eight days, but that same success might hinge on *Boon's* being able to use her torpedo tubes without restriction. Angell was assuming a responsibility that might have oppressed a timid soul. Having reached his decision, he could await the next development without qualms.

The swing shift had arrived for work by the time George reported that the planners had come on board.

"I had to give orders to the gangway watch to stop that work by any necessary means, sir," explained George. "The snapper of the new gang had his job orders given him, and nothing else would stop him."

"Very well," said Angell; he was already on his way aft. A thin rain was falling again, and a cold wind was blowing, and darkness was closing in round the brilliantly lighted yard. Tempers might well be short in these unpleasant conditions. The three planners had their coat collars turned up and their hands thrust deep into their pockets.

"You understand my difficulty, gentlemen?" asked Angell.

There on deck there was a keener sense of reality than existed in a comfortable office with a ship's plan laid out on a table, and the third dimension of height assumed its due importance in relation to length and breadth.

"A time may come when you'll need these guns like hell," said one of the planners.

"I don't doubt it," said Angell, "but—"

Standing there in the chill wind, all five of them had momentary visions. Some of them could picture the *Boon* wheeling over a tossing sea, raining death down upon the unseen menace forty fathoms below; this deck would be full of men then, hurrying the ponderous depth charges from the magazines to maintain the bombardment. Angell passed from that picture to another—of *Boon* swinging to deliver a salvo of torpedoes and being baulked by those guns at a crucial moment.

"Put 'em farther aft, here, and you'll have sufficient clearance," said another planner.

"Yes," replied Angell; and then he said that unpleasant word he had already used once, "but—" He was visualising something else now, no imaginary battle picture, but the plan of the deck below. "Send for the chief engineer," he said abruptly to George.

It took less than two minutes for Lieutenant Borglum to report, uncomfortable at the transition from his warm engine room to the chilly deck.

"What do you have under here?" demanded Angell.

Borglum pondered the question for five seconds. "Main electrical distribution board," he said.

"I was afraid so," said the planner who had hardly spoken as yet.

"No good then," said another.

They could all smile at that moment, at the thought of what would happen to every electrical circuit in the ship if the main distribution board were subjected to the ponderous shock of a K gun hurling a depth charge a hundred feet into the air.

"It'll have to be right aft then," said the first planner. "What do you say, captain?" They moved to the designated spot. "This was the original idea. But the men'll have the devil of a time getting round."

"So they will," agreed Angell. "But this is the place, for sure."

He thought of the bunks being put up at this moment in the crowded mess halls for the additional hands, of the sweltering heat of a blacked-out ship in the tropics, and then of bursting shells and blazing oil tanks. A man more ready with words might have uttered a facile epigram to the effect that men were likely to have the devil of a time in war, but that was not the sort of thing Angell was likely to say.

"I'll come down into the wardroom, if I may," said the first planner, "and get this job order altered."

The *Boon* would be able to launch her torpedoes unhampered after all.

And at midnight on the fifth she crept out of Mare Island Navy Yard exactly on time, heading into a strong breeze. Aft the K guns reared their ungainly shapes; at the mast forward the radar antenna revolved absurdly. Ranged round the upper deck were the new twenty-millimetre guns that experience had shown would be necessary—would hardly be sufficient —to deal with aerial attack. There were the changes visible at a glance from shore, but all through the ship the differences were fantastic. Ready-service ammunition boxes had been built in. There were literally miles of new wires installed for the degaussing gear and elsewhere, so that electrically she was a different ship.

The personnel had changed just as profoundly. Two officers had left the ship, and three had come to replace them; half the crew had left, and twice as many new men had come on board. The peacetime designers who had built *Boon* ten years ago believed then that they had packed the hull with every possible means of defence and offence, manned by as many men as could live in Spartan discomfort on board. Yet, somehow, space had been found for the new weapons, and the men would have to endure sub-Spartan discomfort, packed together with never a chance of a moment's privacy, three men sleeping where two had before been crowded. The cooking arrangements called for the most careful organisation to insure that each twenty-four hours each man had enough to eat; the fresh water, which had just sufficed before, now had to be limited and rationed, and water hours had to be instituted.

But the new weapons, the new officers and the new men were here in the ship, steaming out to sea after that incredible eight days—the first and earliest proof that the giant which was the United States was gathering his strength together. The officers and men who had been left behind would serve as a nucleus round which fresh drafts could be assembled and trained. They, in time to come, would be ready to act as nuclei themselves, and with the unbelievable American productive capacity turning out new construction more and more rapidly, the giant's strength could increase in geometric progression, beginning

115

slowly, but multiplying itself a hundred-fold in a few years.

In a few years? Singapore had fallen; the enemy were in Rangoon; the pathetic fragments of Allied naval strength in Indonesia had been annihilated in the Java Sea, and now the tide of conquest was reaching out to New Guinea. Rommel had reached the frontier of Egypt, Hitler was within two marches of Moscow, and the U-boats were sinking merchant ships four times as fast as they could be replaced. The slow beginning might perhaps mean that the giant would never be able to exert that giant's strength.

Yet a convoy was completing in the darkness within the Golden Gate awaiting the dawn, to bear the first new elements of American strength out into the Pacific. And here was the *Boon*, steaming out through the net defences, as the winking lights ordered, and breathing defiance.

As she quickened her pace, there rang through the ship the first ping of the sonar apparatus, searching for submarine enemies. Twenty thousand times a day *Boon* would probe the depths, for a thousand days still to come, if she should live so long. Angell, on the bridge, felt the *Boon*'s bows lift and surge as she met the Pacific swell, and the westerly breeze roared round him in the night. The spray came hurtling aft, yet all this was not sufficient to drown a new strange sound that reached his ears as he stood on the wing of the bridge. The *Boon* met the next roller and heaved her bows higher and hung for a moment; and when she tossed up her stern as she slid down the slope, the sound was repeated. It was a human chorus, a groan, a catcall, half apprehensive and half defiant, half humorous and half involuntary. There were close to a hundred men on board who had never in their lives until this moment felt the surge and heave of the sea under their feet, and they were still so insufficiently imbued with the spirit of discipline as to think it natural to give vent to the emotions they were feeling. Angell rasped out an order which would impress on the crew that this was not the case.

He turned to look aft through the roaring darkness, but there was nothing to be seen, not even the blacked-out outline of the coast of California receding behind him. He found Klein, the communications officer, beside him peering aft as well.

"We're still heading out from the coast, sir?"

"Yes."

"I thought so, sir. But—"

"But?"

"On the screen we have the outline dead ahead."

"You're getting the radar lined up?"

"Yes, sir. This is the first chance we've had."

"Keep on trying," said Angell.

"Aye aye, sir."

An unexpected wave on the starboard bow caused the *Boon* to shudder and lurch and roll. Then she put her bows up again, hung and shot steeply down. With the change of slope came clatterings and thumpings; Angell had been listening for them. In the quiet of a harbor everything could be made as secure as apparently everything could possibly be, but the first bit of wind and sea would always reveal the falsity of that assumption. A tenth of an inch of play would become an inch after the first wave. That

117

inch could become a foot in five minutes, and that foot could mean destruction and ruin in half an hour. There were fenders dragging at their lashings and boats stirring uneasily against the gripes and the strongbacks. More dangerous still, there was subtle movement among the depth charges packed in aft in what had once been the deck-gear locker.

Angell could see Antonini, the first lieutenant, hurrying round the deck with his damage-control party, working with shaded lights to make everything secure. A crash and clatter from below told that the galley staff, as ever, had been caught napping; pots and pans which had seemed in harbor to be perfectly safely put away always fell in cascades with the first experience of the open sea. Cooks never seemed to learn that lesson.

Cousin George loomed up on the bridge beside him. "The shortest shakedown cruise on record, sir," he said. "Four hours before the convoy comes out through the Gate."

"It's a seven-knot convoy," said Angell. "Thirteen days to Pearl. That's long enough to make something of this ship."

The *Boon* slid down a slope and hit the trough with a shattering thump, sending a shower of spray, invisible in the darkness, back over the bridge.

"We'll have to work 'em hard, sir," said George.

"We can—and we will," said Angell.

"It won't be any trouble with this lot, sir. They're as keen as if their lives depended on it. So they do, of course."

Then came thirteen days of drills and exercises, thirteen days in which the amorphous crew could

118

crystallise into an efficient body—a team reacting to orders without a wasted second or a wasted movement—while the convoy wallowed along behind them on its eternal zigzag course. They could not be thought of as days of monotony. The work was too hard and too varied for that, despite the constant repetition; and even the rebels and the stupid men could not help being aware of the steady progress made, as well as of the fact that their lives might at any moment depend on their prompt action. It was easy to remember the confusion of the first general quarters —confusion despite the warning of the loudspeakers: "This is a drill. All hands will proceed at a walk." Half the hands forgot the rule to go up ladders on the starboard side and down them on the port, but Seaman Second Class Cohen would never forget for the rest of his life that he was very properly ascending a starboard ladder at a walk when he met three large seamen who were not merely improperly descending but doing so on the double.

There was satisfaction, as the days went by, in reaching one's station in the minimum time with the minimum of confusion, and satisfaction in a prompt report to the bridge of the station's being manned and ready. There was satisfaction in taking one's place in the gun mount and feeling it train round, ready for action. Habit did more; it made the crowded mess decks more bearable even to the born solitaries among the crew, so that the precious interior life could be resumed, and habit inured the sensitive souls to the rough-and-tumble talk of the lower deck. There were incidents to distinguish one day from

119

another—the firing with live ammunition at the red weather balloon released from the upper deck, the whole ship pulsating with the recoil of the guns and the thunder of the discharges echoing in the ear. There was the incident when Torpedoman Third Class Constantinidi, during a drill, was ordered to "simulate firing the K gun". He did not know what the word "simulate" meant, but he knew by now how to fire a K gun, and the startled convoy had to be reassured when, before their bows, the depth charge soared into the air, to plunge into the sea with a rumbling explosion and a fountain of black water.

Lieutenant Klein, the communications officer, toiling away at the manuals of the radar set with the help of Radioman First Class Alvarez and a team of assistants who, like him, had never seen a radar set in their lives before, had the satisfaction of seeing the convoy make a vague appearance on his screen. It was the earliest type of air-search radar; and to pick up a surface target called for a range of two miles, and even then with inferior results. But the only possible target on which he could exercise himself and his men was the convoy, and he made the most of the opportunities granted him when Angell took the *Boon* out ahead of the convoy to exercise his range-finder and gunnery-control crews upon it— those wallowing ships were the innocent target of every weapon on board the destroyer.

That was not all by any means; for on the eighth morning out, Alvarez suddenly demanded Klein's attention to the screen. "There's a pip here, sir."

So there was. Klein looked at the vague apparition illuminated by the revolving ray. It was really not such a vague apparition—it was a definite pip, an aircraft, and it was approaching, coming up from far astern. Klein stared at the thing for another second, during which he somehow contrived to remember all the freaks and misbehaviour of that set during the past week. It was a pip for certain, and Klein wasted no time. He dashed out on to the bridge from the captain's sea cabin, wherein the radar had been installed. Harper had the deck; he was supervising the training of a new helmsman at the wheel, but Angell was on the bridge within earshot.

"Aircraft bearing zero nine five!" said Klein. "Approaching!"

There was another second's pause as Angell weighed the information. They were eight hundred miles from the Islands—it could not be a search plane from Oahu. Three months ago a Japanese carrier force had crept unseen within striking range of Pearl Harbor; the attacking planes had been spotted on a radar screen, but disaster had ensued when the report was not acted upon. There might be a Japanese carrier force somewhere out over the horizon, heading for the Coast, possibly. This could be a search plane.

"Sound general quarters," said Angell. "This is not a drill."

"This is not a drill," repeated the loudspeakers as the alarm blared. "This is not a drill."

The men came pouring to their stations, steel helmets clattering. Talkers plugged in their earphones; the helmsman under training was relieved at the wheel and hurried off to his station. Angell fought down the excitement which was making him swallow hard; he compelled himself to take notice of the

121

details. There was some confusion, and he could see trouble at the forward gun mounts. That must be corrected. But Klein, fat equable Klein, was showing up well.

"Aircraft bearing zero nine five," came his report. "Course two five five!"

So the aircraft had laid a course directly for them.

"Course zero zero zero," ordered Angell. He would have every possible gun bearing when the plane came in sight. *Boon* rolled deeply as she came round into the trough. The grey sky raced up and down before Angell's binoculars as he strove to pick up the approaching plane. There it was—a speck, a dot, coming right at them. It would hit the convoy first.

"That's the Pan Am Clipper from San Francisco," said Antonini, beside him, and then remembered to add, "sir".

Angell recognised the profile a moment later—it was quite unmistakable—and cousin George confimed it by telephone from his station aft. Angell watched it approach while behind him he heard the telephone talkers repeating the reports of stations manned and ready. If that had been a hostile plane, *Boon* would have been practically ready for action by the time it was in range—a satisfactory performance.

Already, by the magic grapevine, the news had gone round the ship. Angell was conscious of a general atmosphere of relaxation, broad grins replacing the tenseness of general quarters. Hands were waved as the plane roared over them, heading westward to the Islands. There was a momentary temptation to clamp down, to remind the crew, cuttingly, that it was their business only to obey orders, but Angell put the thought aside. This was not that sort of crew. These were men who could think for themselves, and this was not the moment to check their enthusiasm. Not for some time yet would it be advisable to tighten up discipline. And it was certainly the moment for a special pat on the back for Lieutenant Klein, who had done his work and shouldered his responsibility like a man. And when that was done, "Secure from general quarters", ordered Angell.

It had been a valuable dress rehearsal. It was a tonic that would relieve for days the tedium of the endless drills and exercises, now that the men knew what it was like to go to their guns with the imminent prospect of using them. There was not time for satiety to be reached before the night when Lieutenant Klein raised the Islands on his screen. An excited crew—half of whom had never before been outside the continental United States—could not be restrained next morning from stealing long glances at romantic Oahu as they approached.

Two Coast Guard cutters on anti-submarine patrol relieved *Boon* of further responsibility for the convoy, and she steamed in the clear light of morning into Pearl Harbor. But it was a sobering experience to see the wrecks of the once proud battleships lying there, and to take a fuel-oil barge alongside with not a single moment wasted. It was sobering to learn that Waikiki Beach was strung with barbed wire—and still more so to learn that liberty, if granted, would last only until sunset, that no men could be on the streets after dark without a special and, indeed, unobtainable pass.

Even before the fuel hoses had been connected, a middle-aged lieutenant commander in work khaki came on board, the inevitable briefcase under his arm, and announced himself as the boarding officer from the headquarters of the commander in chief, Pacific Fleet. At his suggestion Angell received him in his cabin while cousin George was instructed to take all necessary precautions to make sure the discussion was neither interrupted nor overheard. The boarding officer came to the point quickly enough.

"You're a stepchild," he said while he was still unzipping his briefcase.

"I thought so," replied Angell. That meant that the squadron to which *Boon* was attached was somewhere else and that there was no immediate prospect of her joining it; that conferred a certain independence, but it also meant that she had no four-striped commodore to intercede for her with the higher command.

"But you're a stepchild with radar," said the boarding officer. He leaned forward across the table, his eyes fixed on Angell's. "There's something you have to understand, even if you don't like it. The Japs have the edge on us when it comes to night fighting. Their lookouts can see better than ours can in the dark. I don't have to tell you all the reasons for it."

"I can guess," said Angell.

The Japanese Navy during all its life had been inferior numerically to those of the major naval powers and had sought in every direction for means to counterbalance that inferiority. One direction had led to Pearl Harbor; another had led to a concentration of training upon night fighting, in which superior

124

numbers would be at a disadvantage. It was the night battle that was the culmination of their peacetime manoeuvres. Those manoeuvres had always been more extensive, more intensive—and much more expensive—than the democratic governments could prevail upon the taxpayers to pay for. The Japanese seaman, on the average, enlisted for a longer time and spent a greater proportion of that time at sea under simulated battle conditions than did his American counterpart, and the simulated battle conditions laid stress upon night fighting. The multiplication of these factors meant that in a night encounter the Japanese lookout might have ten times as much experience in that duty as had the American. It was an unpalatable truth.

"You're the first destroyer to be fitted with radar," said the boarding officer. "And the Japs haven't any at all—as yet. So you can guess how badly you're wanted out there." The jerk of his head indicated the illimitable wastes of the Western Pacific.

"The quicker the better as far as I'm concerned," said Angell.

"You'll have to take a convoy out with you, all the same," said the boarding officer. "Twelve-knot convoy this time—three transports and a tanker; you'll need to fuel from the tanker, in any case."

"Very well," said Angell. Those words, as usual, meant that there was nothing else to say.

"So here are your orders," went on the boarding officer, bringing papers out of the briefcase.

Those orders took *Boon* out of Pearl Harbor nineteen hours after she had come in—nineteen hours devoted to fuelling, to taking on ammunition for replacement of what had been expended in practice and to cramming her with provisions until every possible corner of the ship was stacked with food.

Three months of war had already doubled the time that the staff's plans contemplated a ship might stay at sea. And now they were in the "forward zone", where an encounter with the enemy was probable rather than possible. That meant "condition watches", with the ship as ready for action and as many men at their stations as was compatible with continued life; discomfort and fatigue pushed to the limits of endurance. It also meant a still keener edge to the drills and exercises. Soon the crew looked back a little shamefacedly on their feelings regarding their voyage to the Islands, which had seemed to them then a high adventure filled with desperate, hard work and all the excitement of novelty. Now they were experienced veterans, they thought, and could remember those early feelings with tolerant amusement.

Boon zigzagged stubbornly out over the endless sea, the convoy astern, the two old four-stack destroyers that constituted the rest of the escort on either quarter, under a sun that grew hotter and hotter and more and more vertical, through rain squalls and flat calms. Above that glittering surface the constantly revolving radar and below it the eternal ping of the sonar searched for the enemy and found nothing, nothing, while the drills and the exercises continued and the mental attitude of the men changed to one of cynical resignation.

Yet, in those desolate wastes, one medium was feverishly busy. The air was charged with messages.

If radar and sonar found nothing, the radio antennas were burdened with news. From Pearl Harbor and Tokyo, Sydney and Singapore, orders and information and occasionally mere nonsense were being poured out, vibrating over the ether in fifty different codes. Those stations whose positions were known and who had therefore no reason for concealment were hard at work. Occasionally, very occasionally, *Boon*'s radiomen found an echo from ships at sea, compelled for one reason or another to reveal their presence. Angell read such of them as Klein was able to take in and decode. It was only the tiniest fraction of the whole, but it was enough to enable Angell to make the deduction, as he told cousin George, that "something big was cooking in the South Pacific".

In a hundred headquarters round the rim of the Pacific, a thousand, perhaps ten thousand, keen minds were at work on that mass of messages, their intuition aided by elaborate machines—analysing, guessing, referring to vast earlier files, gaining a grain of sense here and a fresh indication there, as two nations endeavoured each to read the other's mind and secrets. Victory or defeat could hinge—not merely could hinge, but would—on rapid deductions regarding the enemy's intentions, when iron-nerved commanders in chief made their decisions based on these necessarily partial deductions and massed their forces to strike at the weak points.

It was one such series of deductions that changed *Boon*'s course. The bored radioman on duty suddenly heard, clear and loud, in the dots and dashes that now were as familiar to him as print, "To *Boon* for action", and applied himself with sudden vigour to recording the coded message, string after string of meaningless groups. It was so long a message, despite the conventional wording, that Klein began to put it through the decoding machine before the end was reached. And the shape and sense that those groups assumed in their passage through the machine sent Klein's plump body into convulsions of excitement in his chair. He did his best to hold himself still as Angell read it when he took it to him.

Angell looked up into his face at the completion of the reading. "Thank you, Mr. Klein," he said.

Those four words were a tremendous compliment. With some officers it might have been necessary to add, "Keep this under your hat", or, "Don't mention this to anyone else", but Angell knew there was no need to say this to Klein, and Klein was deeply appreciative. He was in possession of a secret for which the Japanese Government would have gladly paid ten million dollars—more tempting, perhaps, he was in possession of information which, divulged even partially, in hints and circumlocutions, would have made him the object of flattering attention in the wardroom.

No more than three minutes later, the signalman on the bridge received a written form from Angell's own hand and trained his light upon the tanker at the head of the convoy.

"Request permission to fuel and proceed on mission assigned."

Then, for an hour *Boon* wallowed beside the tanker while the hoses topped up her bunkers to the last inch, and rude comments were shouted across the foaming gap from one crew to another—each keyed up by the welcome sight of new faces after days of monotony. Then she cast off and headed away, acknowledging the commodore's signal of good luck. That hour gave birth to the wildest rumors. The radioman who had taken in the signal, "To *Boon* for action", and the signalman who had sent Angell's message naturally told all they knew. The rumour that received most general acceptance was to the effect that *Boon* had been ordered back not merely to Pearl but all the way to San Francisco.

Angell told the news to cousin George; they spoke in low voices in Angell's cabin. The fewer people who knew how much could be read of the Japanese codes the better—a casual word dropped in a New Zealand bar might result a month later in those codes being changed and the whole weary work having to be done again. But cousin George must be told, for, in war, life is even more uncertain that appendicitis and cerebral haemorrhage and coronary occlusion can make it. If Angell were to die, cousin George must be ready to go on with the plan.

Angell marked a small cross on the chart spread out on his desk. "That's a Japanese heavy cruiser," he said, and George whistled as Angell gave the latitude and longitude. "She had engine trouble, and the big convoy she was with left her behind—I told you there was something cooking in the South Pacific."

"Now she's on her way again?" asked George.

"It looks like it. It isn't just the intercepts that say so. One of our subs spotted her—couldn't get in an attack, as she was going twenty-five knots, but she made sure of her course and speed. That's where she was, and this is where she's going."

"And we can cut her off," said George decisively. "My calculation is that we can do it with five hours to spare. I'd like you to confirm my working."

"Aye aye, sir," said George.

They shared momentarily a memory of an incident of years ago, when Angell had been a gunnery-division officer on a cruiser, and George, a new and very junior officer, had been sent off as boat officer on a liberty trip to the landing; the cruiser lay anchored in a fog at Long Beach, and Angell had the deck watch. George, while returning, had come across a Navy boat, drifting, with a broken-down engine, forlornly out to sea before wind and tide. He had taken her in tow. That Long Beach fog was so thick that one could not see his hand before his face, and the process of taking the other boat in tow consumed minutes, during which they had been swept a considerable and almost incalculable distance seaward. But George had worked out the tricky navigation problem in his head and had brought his boat back neatly to the cruiser's side at the first try. He could be trusted with a simple problem in interception.

Angell was tapping with the butt of his pencil on the chart, but he did not take his eyes from George's. "We'll make contact at night," he said.

"And that's just as well," answered George. In a daylight battle *Boon* would not stand one chance in a hundred against a heavy cruiser. "We ought to bring something off at that rate."

"We'll come in on her bow and launch a spread," supplemented Angell.

They might be two business partners discussing the technique of some contemplated deal. But they were staking their lives and not their fortunes, and the profit would be death and wounds and agony—and the lives they were risking were their own, while the profit would be their country's.

"Klein's doing good work with the radar, sir," said George. "No need to tighten things up there."

"I think you're right," agreed Angell. "Well, let me have a finer course, if you can, than the one I've set."

"Aye aye, sir."

They left the cabin, and *Boon* continued on her way. The convoy was already hull down as they came on deck, and soon they were alone, rolling deeply now as the Pacific swell came in almost broad on the beam. The sun sank sullenly into a cloud-bank over the quarter, and night closed in upon the darkened ship. On deck, men suddenly felt a passionate desire to smoke cigarettes now that it was impossible. Below decks, men off watch sweltered in the suffocating embrace of the sticky heat which closed in upon them with the darkening of the ship. So she went on, wallowing over the swell, through the night until dawn, through the day until dusk, four hundred miles from where she left the convoy. Somewhere during those four hundred miles she crossed two invisible lines—not lines of longitude or latitude, and no one could have ruled them with certainty on a chart, as they were lines that fluctuated from day to day with the movements of fleets and with the establishment of land bases for air power. Beyond the first line lay no man's land—no man's water—and beyond the second lay that part of the Pacific where the Japanese navy rode unchallenged. The American raider there had to be swift and furtive like *Boon,* or overwhelmingly strong, like a fleet, or submersible like a submarine.

The second evening closed round *Boon* in a flurry of rain squalls; the sonar was still pinging fruitlessly, the radar antennas still rotating without picking up the least indication of friend or foe—it could only be foe in these waters. An hour after sunset Angell came on to the darkened bridge to where Carlsen had the deck.

"Steer a base course of zero one three, Mr. Carlsen," he said.

"Zero one three. Aye aye, sir."

It was as simple as that—one brief order and one brief acknowledgement. There was no hint of the thirty hours of anxiety through which Angell had lived, nor of Carlsen's astonishment at this remarkable change of course. Carlsen could hardly help guessing now that something was in the wind; but to nine tenths of the individuals on board, by now one course was the same as another. These veterans of a month at sea had already acquired an almost Oriental fatalism. Now *Boon* was squarely in the path of the Japanese cruiser—if Angell's calculations were correct. She should be two hundred miles to the northeastward, and with the two ships travelling at a combined speed of forty knots they should make contact in five hours—less than that.

Angell felt an uncontrollable surge of hot blood

under his skin as he thought about it. He had felt that same thing several times that day already, but now he found himself shaking with excitement as well. He mastered the trembling with a supreme effort of will—that was merely for his own self-respect, because in the utter darkness of the wing of the bridge no one else could see it. Not even a lifetime spent at sea, not even a thousand encounters with responsibility and danger, could condition a man for this supreme adventure.

"Come right to zero two three, Mr. Carlsen."

"Zero two three. Aye aye, sir."

Angell was sending *Boon* on a long zigzag up the predicted course of the cruiser; it was the best allowance he could make for slight errors of navigation by either vessel. With that done, he settled himself in his chair on the bridge. He knew he should rest, but he had neither intention nor expectation of going to sleep. In consequence, with everything done that needed to be done, sleep crept up on him, and he dozed lightly until a footstep roused him.

"Are you going to general quarters, sir?" George had shown up beside him on the bridge.

"I'll do that when they relieve the watch," answered Angell and noted with interest that the first hint of practical detail was sufficient to steady him.

The *Boon* slithered over the invisible sea, rolling heavily in the trough. It was the blackest imaginable night, heavily overcast—thank God. Angell became aware that George was peering at his wrist watch, and the moment prompted him to do the same. It was incredible that fifty minutes had passed since he altered course—incredible too, now that he was waiting, to find how long the next ten minutes lasted.

"Come left to zero one three," he ordered.

"Zero one three. Aye aye, sir."

"I want," began Angell to George, and then he stopped to cough and clear his throat. Excitement was making him hoarse. "I want you to be ready to keep the plot when we make contact—if we do. Don't go to your regular station. Stay by the telephone beside Klein."

"Aye aye, sir. I think you're quite right, if you'll pardon me, sir."

Why did not George show any sign of buck fever? Or was he doing so? Angell suddenly understood George's constrained formality and felt very much better. There was nothing like seeing other people under strain to gain relief oneself.

Now the watch was changing. "Sound general quarters," said Angell.

The alarm blared through the ship. There was sudden noise and bustle, the inevitable clanking of steel helmets, voices raised here and there. Angell found himself taking a mental note that he must mention that tomorrow to his officers. Tomorrow? Silence fell upon the ship again except for the quiet wording of the reports. Now she was silent as well as invisible upon the invisible sea. She was ready for instant action now, ready for battle at a moment's notice. Her fighting capacity was at its highest pitch, but it would not stay at that level for long. Men would grow tired and sleepy. Men would grow careless. He must conserve the ship's strength during the long vigil; he gave another order to George.

"Aye aye, sir," said George, turning away after an invisible salute.

"Now hear this," bellowed the loudspeaker five seconds later. "Now hear this."

George's voice took over from there. This was not a drill, he said. The ship was passing through a zone of extreme danger, but as the period was likely to be prolonged, officers at each station could detail half their men in turn to sleep at their stations.

Now it was also time to alter course again. "Come right to zero two three."

Now everything was ready until the next change of course in an hour's time. There was nothing more to be done—nothing, that is, except to wait, wait, wait, standing in that utter darkness, resolutely keeping the mind from imagining mistakes and disaster.

Old Flower, the senior quartermaster, was standing by the wheel now, supervising a quartermaster striker, but ready to take over when necessary. He was a man of immense experience and of reliable stolidity, but he had seen no more war than Angell had—would he be as stolid as that and as dependably obedient if shells were raining on the ship and the decks spouting flames? And he himself? No, he could, and should, wonder about Flower, but he must not wonder about himself. *Perhaps*—

"Bridge aye," said a talker in the darkness.

This was it! This was it!

"Skunk bearing zero zero two!" It was Klein's report from the radar. "Range seventeen thousand yards!"

A rain squall was bursting over the ship at this very moment, but Angell was unaware of it. Now was the time for instant orders to be given. Now was the time when, after all the hours of waiting, every second was of importance. A clear head was needed to give orders in logical sequence, a quick mind to give them without waste of time.

"Mind your helm. Steer a tight course."

"I have the wheel steady on zero two three, sir." That was Flower.

"All bridge talkers—alert all hands to stand by for action. Prepare for torpedo attack . . . Lieutenant Brown, let me have that course."

"Aye aye, sir. Target bearing zero zero zero! Range sixteen thousand yards!" Ships on collision courses came together with paralysing rapidity.

"Prepare for torpedo attack to port."

"Aye aye, sir," from Antonini, moving to the port torpedo director. That order and that reply had been given a hundred times before in drill, but this was the real thing, no simulated play acting, but war— life and death.

"Target bearing three five five! Range fourteen five."

Now from George, "Course three one five will bring us in on her port bow."

"Left full rudder. Steady up on three one five . . . Talker, alert the lookouts to keep sharp lookout ahead."

The first contact had been made toward the very end of one leg of the zig-zag—the best proof of how necessary the zigzag course had been.

"Disengage gyro stops." That was Antonini at the torpedo director again, giving the definitive order that would make the torpedoes ready for action. He was speaking with funereal solemnity—perhaps that was the best way to insure against mistakes, at the same time restraining the excitement of the men who would have to obey those orders.

"Target bearing three five four! Range eleven thousand yards!"

They must be very nearly on the correct course, if not dead upon it. Klein's next report would show.

"Cap'n, can you tell me what's the target?" Antonini was asking the question.

"Heavy cruiser."

"Two-degree spread," ordered Antonini in that lugubrious voice, so unlike his normal conversation. "Set running depth fifteen feet."

Down aft in the black darkness, men would be making those adjustments; steady fingers and unhurried calm there were as vitally necessary as a clear head on the bridge.

"Target bearing three five three steady. Range nine thousand!"

So they were dead on course, running on a constant bearing straight to meet the target.

"Match pointers," said Antonini and then, in a tone only a trifle less flat, "Setup complete, cap'n."

"Very well."

"Target bearing three five three. Range eight thousand yards."

Now everything was done—everything was ready for the attack.

"All engines ahead flank," ordered Angell.

"All engines ahead flank," repeated the hand at the telegraph, but there was a crack in his voice as he spoke. "Engine room answers. All engines ahead flank."

That man would bear careful watching; but the sudden tremendous increase in vibration and the audible rise in the pitch of the blowers' note told that he had carried out his order correctly. *Boon* was charging in now, hurtling over the water at optimum speed to close the gap in the briefest possible time.

"Radar, let me have consecutive ranges."

"Range seven thousand yards."

The rain squall had ceased—Angell could not remember when. It was a pity that it had done so, but it was far too much to hope for—that they could have come all the way in under cover of a squall.

"Range six five hundred."

But the night was still utterly black. Angell, peering out with straining eyes through his binoculars over the starboard bow, could see nothing at all. But perhaps the famous Japanese lookouts had spotted the *Boon*. Perhaps already there were alarms blaring over there, a helm being put over to foil his thrust, guns being trained for their destruction.

"Range six thousand yards."

Only two minutes—one minute now. He could not see the enemy even though he knew where to look. Could the Japs see them—were conditions more favourable to them? But even when they did, there would be a lapse of time; time would pass while they made sure, while the information was passed on, while it was being digested and acted upon.

"Range five five double oh."

"Target spotted, cap'n," said Antonini.

"Gun director reports on target," said a talker out of the darkness.

Now he could see it—a solid nucleus of greater darkness in the otherwise uniform dark, still too vague for him to guess at her course. But if he could see them, then almost for certain they could see him. How long before they reacted?

"Range four five double oh."

He would wait a little longer—just a little longer, before he swung to parallel the cruiser. He had a momentary vision of the layout of the afterdeck to complement his mental plan of the coming turn. Thank God he had had those K guns moved—he could loose his whole salvo without any restraint at all. Was that dark form changing its shape?

"Right full rudder. Come to zero one five."

Boon lay right over as the rudder bit into the sea and swung her round.

"Mark!" said Antonini sharply.

"On target!" from the operator.

"Fire when ready!" said Angell. No one noticed, not even himself, how his voice cracked as he spoke.

The ready light glowed on the director.

"Fire one!" said Antonini, using his funeral tone again. The two monosyllables were moments of harsh reality in this mad unreality of shrieking blowers and foaming water and heeling decks. But Antonini was still speaking, and what he was saying in that flat voice now blended with the madness.

"If I hadn't been a torpedo officer, I wouldn't be here," said Antonini slowly.

139

"Fire two! If I hadn't been a torpedo officer, I wouldn't be here. Fire three!"

So he droned on, inhumanly, as eight torpedoes were being fired. Drill had taught him that the recital consumed the thirty-five seconds desirable in firing a spread. It was the same method and almost the same words as had been used in firing salutes to Nelson or John Paul Jones.

"Fire eight!" said Antonini and, still without a change of tone, "All torpedoes expended, sir. No casualties."

"Very well." He had completed a mission to the best of his ability; this was a peak, an Everest, in his professional career, with eight torpedoes launched at a rich target. But this was no moment to relax, in these last fleeting seconds before those torpedoes hit —or missed.

"Steady on zero one five," reported Flower at the wheel.

"Main battery commence firing!" ordered Angell, and the words were hardly out of his mouth before the five-inch guns burst out in a shattering crash and great jets of flame.

The guns were on the target, the range was ludicrously short. Because the Japs must certainly have seen the flashes as the powder charges hurled the torpedoes over the side, there was no need for further concealment—there could be no doubt that the cruiser's guns were training round upon *Boon* at this very moment. Angell must hit her while he might, doing what damage he could before she sank him if all those eight torpedoes had missed.

The flashes were blinding. *Boon* was shaking convulsively under the recoils. Still he must keep his head clear. "Fishtail her, Flower!" he yelled through the din.

"Fishtail. Aye aye, sir," Flower's voice answered him, barely audible.

The twenty-millimetres were at work too, scarlet tracers threading the dark. They stood no chance of hitting, but Angell checked himself on the point of ordering them to cease fire. *Let 'em,* he said to himself.

The cruiser was suddenly illuminated with bursts of fire as the shells rained upon her, and then illuminated again with huge horizontal spouts of flame —that was her big guns firing straight at the *Boon.* And then another, different, flame appeared at the cruiser's water line, abaft her after turret. Then the flash of a five-inch, bursting close above, illuminated a soaring fountain of spray beside the cruiser.

"A hit!" That was Antonini, shouting at the top of his lungs.

The deck heeled madly; the great spouts of flame again came from the cruiser's guns, and then another dull burst of flame flashed at her water line, below her stacks.

"Another hit!" yelled Antonini.

Over went the deck again as *Boon* fishtailed; some of the din died away as the twenty-millimetres ceased to bear. A sheet of flame went soaring up the cruiser's side, lighting up her every detail, and flying and blazing fragments indicated small internal explosions. The cruiser was dropping astern of the *Boon* —it was not merely a relative change of position due to the fishtailing. Her engines must have stopped and now there was another explosion on her water line, well forward.

"Three hits!" yelled Antonini and then, in his flat voice, "I wish to report three hits, sir."

Everything that Angell could see of the cruiser had changed. He realised that she had swung nearly bows-on to him and she was listing right over. Her very upper works seemed different—perhaps a mast had fallen. And there was not a sign of life about her amid the flames. She had fired only those two salvos, which had gone heaven knew where.

"Cease firing," he ordered. "All engines ahead two thirds. Right standard rudder. Bring her round again."

The dead silence, the sudden diminution of the whine of the blowers, the total cessation of the jarring of the guns, the dying down of the wind of their passage—all this was in fantastic contrast to the din of a moment ago. He could even hear the sound of the waves under the bow, and the ping of the sonar—it was like any one of a score of recent nights at sea. But he became conscious of the sound of the flames and the explosions in the cruiser, and the waves round her were red with reflected light. Fires glowed through her steel. Antonini crossed the bridge to keep her under observation.

"She's going, sir. She's going!"

The blazing structure was heeling over more and more; there was a roar of quenched metal and a cloud of steam as she lowered her red-hot side down into the water. In a haze of smoke and vapor her bows reared up skyward as her stern sank deeper; her bows were almost bottom up and still there were flames and explosions. Then she slid backward slowly, foot by foot, and the fires went out as the sea closed over her, leaving Angell staring with dazzled eyes that could see nothing at all in the ink-black night. And there was not a sound through the length and breadth of the *Boon*—only a stony silence, the silence of awe.

"All engines ahead one third," said Angell.

The riven corpse of the cruiser was sinking through the black waters of the Pacific, down to the ooze a thousand fathoms deep, and Angell was speaking like a man come back to consciousness after delirium. Everything was crystal clear, yet unbelievable.

"Prepare to rescue survivors."

He had delivered the first counterstroke. The world would know now, the Japanese would realise with apprehension, that the giant was recovering his strength. Staffwork and production, training and doctrine, ingenuity and common sense—all these factors had played a part in the victory.

The Japanese could fight on and could die, but their deaths would be unavailing.

They would be as unavailing as the deaths of the few men whom *Boon* found afloat as she crept forward through the debris of the sunken cruiser—men who beat off the hands stretched to rescue them, the man on the life raft who shot at his would-be saviours with a pistol and who was left drifting in the lonely Pacific, the men who submerged themselves voluntarily rather than be picked up. Useless deaths these were, but life seemed valueless even to the four spiritless creatures who huddled in the *Boon*'s mess hall after being pulled out of the water. Perhaps they could foresee a future of defeat.

U.S.S. *Cornucopia*

The identity of the individual who decided on the name *Cornucopia* for the Submarine Depot Ship in which the supply officer served is hidden deep in the recesses of the Navy Department, but the name is startlingly appropriate, for she is a fount of plenty. Men who do not serve in her think her the ugliest ship that has been designed since Noah went into the business, and they may be right. On the after end she carries a couple of monstrous cranes that never fail to call forth bad language from the signal ratings on the superstructure forward when they try to read signals from the ship following her; and whenever the captain puts his engines astern he has to rely on Providence—as well as on an officer stationed on the fan tail with a telephone—to keep her tail out of mischief. Her silhouette bulges here and there as if streamlining had never been thought of, and it is only when one realises that she is capable, literally, of inflating balloons at one end while refuelling less capacious ships at the other end that one forgives her unsightly lines.

Far more than a thousand blue-jacketed men live on board her, and far more than half of them are skilled mechanics trained to use the precision machines set up in the workshops which take up a great deal of her cubic capacity. Her boast is that she can do any repair job she may be called upon to do, supply any part, replace any consumable stores, with special and particular reference to submarines.

The theory that dictated the construction of U.S.S. *Cornucopia* and her ugly sisters—*Proteus* and others—is that she should constitute an advanced naval base in herself. In the dark days when the Japanese were moving southward down the Pacific, capturing island after island, somebody had the vision to foresee that the tide would turn, and the moral courage to make preparations for that moment. So the *Cornucopia* was ready as soon as islands began to be reconquered; she steamed in before even the Seabees could begin their work of constructing shore installations and could take up her work of servicing and repairing the moment her anchor touched bottom in coral lagoon or malarious roadstead.

Not merely that, but as Uncle Sam advances, as he proceeds not merely to reconquer but to conquer, to tear from the Japanese hold islands which have long been treasured possessions of the Rising Sun, *Cornucopia* can go forward with him. There is no need to leave anything behind; she has everything inside her already, and it is only a matter of hauling up her anchor and proceeding northwestward under the protecting shield of the sea power which, like a gigantic boa constrictor, is slowly crushing the life out of the Japanese Empire.

The circle of Japanese dominations grows smaller while it grows weaker, but there still remains a wide area into which the surface ships of the United

Nations can only penetrate spasmodically if at all, and it is in this area that the Japanese are most sensitive to attack, for it is over these waters that their lines of communication run, dependent upon their attenuated mercantile marine and their rather rapidly dwindling escort vessels.

Submarines are delicate pieces of machinery; parts wear out and break down, and even if the crews can stand the strain of operating them and can maintain them in seagoing condition, there comes a time when the last torpedo is fired or food and fuel begin to run short and they must return to fill up. The less time they spend on passage the sooner they are back at work again; and now, happily, Pearl Harbor and Australia are far from the waters in which they operate. So instead of bringing them back to Honolulu, Uncle Sam moves Honolulu out to them—at least, not Honolulu, but U.S.S. *Cornucopia* and her sisters, which, according to the proud boast of the men who man the depot ships, are just as good.

And this brings us to my friend the supply officer, whom I mentioned in the first sentence of this story and have since neglected in favour of a digression on the sea power which it is his duty to put into practice. No one looking at him, at his rosy cheeks and innocent spectacles, could imagine that in him sea power is embodied. His appearance never sets one's mind running on Nelson or Mahan. No one, for that matter, would believe him to be forty-five, which he is, and no one observing his unwrinkled brow would ever credit him with the vast experience which he possesses in the ways and tricks of submarines, their habit of burning out the most unheard-of accessories, and the habit of their captains of demanding stores and spare parts in quantities that would make a less experienced man gasp and of a nature that would stagger one less familiar with the contents of his storerooms.

Twenty-six thousand items the supply officer is prepared to supply; twenty thousand that may be in demand by any ship in the Navy, and six thousand peculiar to submarines. Twenty-six thousand items, from the things that anyone could think of, like battery acid and fuel oil and torpedoes and shells, like baking powder and preserved milk and canned fruit, down to recondite things like "Hinges, Butt, Marine-use Type B 2030 D (full surface fast)" and Salinometer Pots and Portable Continuous-acting Tachometers. Twenty-six thousand items, from washers to gyro-compasses. Submarines never casually throw rubbish overboard—it might float and reveal their presence. Instead, they tie it up in burlap bags and sink it overside, and the supply officer has to see to it that there are burlap bags for the purpose; and as in a submarine everything is precious and there is nothing casually to hand which could be spared as a sinker, the supply officer has to supply sinkers in the form of lumps of concrete.

He not merely has to have these things, but he has to be able to lay his hand on any one of them at a moment's notice; they must be not merely card-indexed but labelled and stored in exact order so that sea power is not hampered by the necessity of waiting while a storekeeper hunts through his stock. A department store is no more complex than a submarine depot ship; far less so, in point of fact, for a department store never has to up anchor and start out to sea in the face of typhoons, and especially never has to be constantly ready to fight off enemies in the air, on the surface and under the sea. Moreover, the department store is never five thousand miles from civilisation, as a submarine depot ship frequently is —as she is intended to be—and if a department store happens to run out of stock it can always send out and buy whatever the exacting customer demands. But if the depot ship runs out of stock of any item she has failed; her supply officer is disgraced in the eyes of the men whom it is his duty to supply, and sea power may have to wait until the deficiency is remedied from a source on the other side of the world. He has to decide maybe a year ahead of time on everything he is likely to be asked for, and having put it into stock, he then has to see to it that it remains in good condition until it is needed.

"But of course," said the supply officer to me, "anything we don't have we can make. That's what our repair shops are for. We cannot merely repair ships, but by golly, we could build 'em if necessary!"

"Did you ever fail?" I asked. "Have they ever wanted anything you couldn't supply?"

In the supply officer's pink baby face a struggle was clearly evident, presumably between the desire for effect and natural truthfulness.

"Be honest," I urged. "Let's hear about it."

So the supply officer told me about the time when U.S.S. *Cornucopia* blotted her copybook. "It was all the result of enemy action," he said in sturdy self-defence.

The enemy action occurred when *Cornucopia* was on her way to an atoll designated as her future anchorage. She is not the sort of ship to court trouble. Despite the guns that bristle on her upper decks, despite her elaborate gunnery-control arrangements and the patience and care which have been devoted to training her gun crews, she must be kept out of harm's way if it is possible; but this time it was not possible. To reach her destination, far forward in the seas which the Japanese for years have thought their own, she and her escort had to pass within range of another island to which the Japanese were still clinging desperately, maintaining it as a base until it should, in the expressive words of an American Admiral, "wither on the bough". As the *Cornucopia* went rolling over the blue Pacific, in "condition two", with half the men resting while the other half manned the guns and the lookout stations, the alarm suddenly pealed through the ship.

"All hands man your battle stations."

Men came pouring up from below, with helmets and lifebelts and gas masks, racing to their battle stations. Each station sent its brief report in over the telephone—"gun one manned and ready", "damage control manned and ready" and so on—and the last report had hardly come in before the Japanese planes were hurtling upon her, and her guns were bellowing in her defence. The blue sky was pock-marked with puffs of black as shells exploded, and red tracers glowed faintly in the dazzling sunshine. *Cornucopia* went through ungainly antics as she swung first to one side and then to the other to disconcert the Japanese aim, and the placid Pacific day

149

was shattered by the roar of the barrage thrown up by escorting destroyers.

In ten minutes the Japanese planes had come and gone, had made their swoop and disappeared, and *Cornucopia* was once more plodding doggedly toward her destination. But she was on fire. A shell from one of the cannons mounted in a Japanese plane had pierced her unprotected side just above the water line close to Frame 84 and, as luck would have it, had started a fire in a compartment crammed with highly combustible stores.

"It might have been a whole lot worse," said the supply officer.

I knew that; *Cornucopia* carried great numbers of torpedoes (how many is a military secret) and mines and ammunition, to say nothing of oil and other combustibles. She might have been blown into tiny fragments—the explosives she carried could lay all Manhattan in ruins. As it was, she had only this one small fire, which blazed furiously for a few moments among those combustible stores before it was put out by the damage-control party. She reached her destination without further incident.

Some Pacific bases have been bitterly disillusioning to the Americans who have garrisoned them, but this atoll was everything a coral island has ever been said to be. There were the dazzling white beaches, the wide circle of coconut palms, the astonishing sapphire-blue of the lagoon in contrast with the paler blue of the surrounding ocean; the sun was not too crushing, the rain not too searching, and mosquitoes were non-existent. For men with time to spare there was fishing; there was the finest surf bathing in the world—everything heart could desire except home. But the crew of *Cornucopia* never had time to spare, because the moment she dropped her anchor inside the lagoon the submarines started coming in, clamouring for attention after their long and dangerous patrols in Japanese waters.

Their crews had nothing to do while they were in— they had hardly laid themselves alongside *Cornucopia* when they were dispatched to the shore to enjoy the fishing and the bathing, the fresh food and the fresh air, and above all, the freedom from the imminent presence of death. Men need rest when they have spent months at a time in the knowledge that they may be killed the next moment, and when every minute of those months they have been thrusting themselves into deadly danger. Not even the elaborate arrangements in a modern American submarine suffice to keep the crews in health on active service; not even the sun-ray lamps and the air conditioning and the carefully planned food.

So when a submarine came into the base her crew could wash their hands of all responsibility and rest on the coral beaches in the shade of the palms, while a substitute crew supplied by *Cornucopia* took charge of their boat. Those enormous cranes which the signalmen so detested would lift them out of the water for repair and cleaning and repainting; skilled ratings would test every bit of the complicated apparatus; worn parts would be replaced and stores renewed. With infinite care fresh torpedoes would be hoisted into the submarines. Shells would be passed down to replace those fired into Japanese shipping, so that by the time the crew was rested and restless again their boat would be ready to go back into Japanese-held waters, to ravage the very coasts of Japan itself, ready for anything.

The twenty-six thousand items *Cornucopia* carried were available to replace any part that had been damaged by wear or by the action of the enemy, and when the unpredictable boats managed to demand something not in stock the *Cornucopia*'s mechanics made it for them. With a supply of every possible metal on board, she could melt her own alloys in her own electric furnace; she could cast the part, and then in her machine-shops she could machine the castings.

But there was one thing missing. Only one, but it was something of the greatest importance, and something—as the supply officer admitted with a lopsided smile—which the *Cornucopia* could neither replace nor make. The original supply had been destroyed in that little fire, and nothing could compensate for the loss.

According to the supply officer, that island paradise was nearly rent asunder by the recriminations of the submarine captains when their requisitions could not be filled. Some of them talked in a lofty tone about morale and the effect of the loss upon the well-being of the crews. Some merely cursed on the grounds of their own personal inconvenience, but in either case their complaints nearly drove the supply officer frantic. They looked on him as personally responsible, and indeed he was—it was no excuse in the eyes of the Navy that that unlucky shell should have landed in a compartment full of highly combustible materials. He could supply anything or he could make anything, so he said, yet here he was denying them an item whose absence could wreck esprit de corps.

"I couldn't supply it and I couldn't make it," said the supply officer pathetically. "That damned shell burned out our whole stock. Twelve thousand rolls of it. Four hundred miles of toilet paper."

December 6th

I know you should not repeat rumours. But people do, and they generally start with the words I have just written, and then they go on, "but I think you ought to know this." I say the same. I know you should not repeat rumours, but I think you ought to know this.

I met them in a bar on Sixth Avenue; I think I noticed them before they noticed me, but there were several reasons why this should be so. One of them was an English soldier, and the English service uniform is still sufficiently conspicuous in New York to attract attention, especially to my eye, which will never, I fear, grow used to its comfortable appearance —almost sloppiness—compared with the uniform of the last war. He was a gunner, as his cap badge showed, not too robust in appearance, and with the dark mobile face of the typical Cockney soldier.

His companion was an American sailor, so huge as to appear twice the size of the Englishman. They made an odd couple, who reminded me at first sight of Lennie and his friend in *Of Mice and Men,* but there was nothing of the half-wit about the big American. Yet there was obviously a bond of affection between the two, a little touching in that Sixth

Avenue bar; as I watched them the thought of *Of Mice and Men* faded completely from my mind. There were even moments when the attitude of the big American toward his lively companion reminded me of a man with a tame monkey.

I had observed them for some time before they noticed me. And the English soldier noticed me first, and the first thing he noticed about me was my shoes. He gave them a casual glance at first, and immediately a closer professional gaze, and then he looked up into my face.

"Englishman, sir?" he asked, and I nodded. "I though so, sir. Hand-made on your own last. Three guineas before the war."

"That's right," I said.

"Oh, gee," said the American, "what's this? Shoes again?"

"You shut up," said the Englishman. "If I didn't know about shoes, you wouldn't be in New York today drinking beer—at least, what you call beer in this country."

"Beer?" said the American. "I'll bet there isn't any better beer than this in Britain. No, sir."

"Don't pay no attention to him, sir," said the gunner. "You know, and I know, sir. But it's no good telling these Americans about beer. Collins is my name, sir. Royal Artillery. But in civil life I sold shoes at Meiklejohn's in Bond Street. You wasn't ever in there, sir, I suppose?"

"I'm afraid not," I said.

"No; those are Barlow's, of course. Good firm, but not as good as mine. You ought to have come to us, sir."

"I will, after the war," I said. "Who's your friend?"

" 'Im? I mean him? Lindstrom's his name."

I told them mine, and the American stood up and shook hands with me.

"Pleased to meet you, sir," he said. "I've read some of your books, I fancy."

That happens to me every now and again, even in a Sixth Avenue bar.

"Books?" said Collins. "You a writer, sir? I'm afraid I haven't read anything of yours, sir."

"Can you read?" said Lindstrom. The little Cockney turned on the big Scandinavian.

"Better than you can in North Carolina."

"North Dakota," said Lindstrom patiently, with a grin at me.

"Same thing," said Collins, and I thought it well to interpose.

"What I want to know," I said, "is what you are doing in New York. What was that that you said about your knowledge of shoes bringing you here?"

"Well," began Collins, and he signalled to the bartender. More beer was before us before I had time to attend to the matter myself. I felt guilty, because I know what an English private soldier's pay amounts to, but Collins reassured me, "That's all right, sir; we've got the money to spend. And that's because I know about shoes, too."

I looked, a little bewildered, from Collins to Lindstrom and back again.

"That's the truth, sir. It was my knowledge of shoes that got us this leave in New York and the money to spend. My knowledge, with a little help from this big lout here."

"Let's have the details," I said.

"It was in Colón, sir—that place at the end of the Panama Canal. Not the place you get the scent from, although I thought it was before I got there. You can buy Eau de Cologne there, all right, but it's not spelled the same."

"What on earth were you doing in Colón?" I asked.

"Gunner, sir, in a freighter. When ships of ours went out through the canal they used drop off us gunners there and we'd pick up another ship to come home in. 'Course, that was before America came in. December sixth, as a matter of fact, this was. The Pacific was safe, and there wasn't a lot of us seagoing gunners. Cristobal's in the Canal Zone, and Colón's outside it in Panama."

I nodded.

"And Colón's a lot livelier than Cristobal is, too! Well, I was in a bar with this boy in blue here, drinking beer, the same as we are now. And we were talking about how we were seeing the world, when in walks one of my push."

"You mean one of the crew that was on your ship?" I asked.

"No, another gunner, same as me. I didn't know him. He gave one look at me and sort of hesitated. Not that I noticed it at the time, but I remembered afterwards. But then he pulled himself together and sat down at a table the other side of the room and called for beer—they think it's beer, out there."

Lindstrom writhed restlessly, but forebore comment.

"We just went on talking, and then I found myself looking at that gunner's boots. It's a habit of mine, sir; I can't never get out of it. Well, those boots

157

weren't never made in England. I looked and I looked, and I said to myself, 'Those boots were made in Germany, or my name's not William Collins.' I looked at that gunner again, and I looked. There wasn't anything wrong with his uniform. That was quite all right. But those boots. Somehow I couldn't swallow them. So I says something about them to this man Lindstrom. It was only casual. It wasn't like asking him if he'd have another pint, but you should have seen what it did to him."

"He didn't see the importance of it, sir," explained Lindstrom, with a tolerant smile. "It's not his canal. And he's not a sailor. I've been taught about the canal ever since I joined."

"Well, what did you do?" I asked.

"He sat up as if someone had pricked him with a pin," said Collins. "He told me to keep my eye on the bloke, and out he went. He came back with the sweat just running off him. It's hot out there in Colón."

"I'd been running," explained Lindstrom. "I'd a buddy I could ask about ships going through the canal. He told me it was all right—the guy was off of the *Duncansby Head*, just come in and waiting to go through the canal."

"But he wasn't satisfied even then," said Collins.

"No, sir," agreed Lindstrom.

"He asked me about those boots again, and we talked about them, and he was still fretting in case he was a spy, when the bloke puts an end to our argument by coming over and sitting down at our table. He'd seen us looking at him and knew we were talking about him. ' 'Ave a drink,' he says, as pleasant as you please. So we has a drink, and we talks for a bit about this and that. He said, like Lindstrom here knew, that he was off the *Duncansby Head*. We'd had a scare as we came over because of a Nazi surface raider in the Atlantic, and I asked him if he had heard anything about her, and he said 'no,' and then we changed the subject. Schoolmaster, he said he was, in civil life. He talked classy, so it might be true, but I didn't like it, all the same. It wasn't quite right. I looked at Lindstrom and tried to tell him so without speaking about it, if you understand me, sir."

"And I saw what he was after," said Lindstrom; "I didn't like the guy any more than he did. And when he asked us to come back to his ship with him—"

"That was fishy, all right," interrupted Collins. "He said he'd got some Scotch, real Scotch, and he wanted us to have a drink. It was funny sitting there, the three of us. I knew he was a phony, all right, and so did Lindy, although we hadn't been able to say a word. And he knew we knew, and he wasn't saying a word either. If we didn't accept, but just let him go back to his ship, we wouldn't be doing our duty."

"That's right," said Lindstrom, "and if he once got us on board—"

Lindstrom made a gesture with a vast hand which hinted significantly at what he thought was likely to happen to them on board.

"He would shut our mouths, all right," said Collins.

"But we had to go along, all the same," remarked Lindstrom. "We just didn't have a chance to settle a thing. All we could do was go along with him like two hicks to a phony crap game."

"Talking pleasant, too," added Collins, "all the

way, until we went up the gangway and found ourselves on board."

The ready flow of speech dried up at this stage and the two looked a little self-conscious.

"For heaven's sake," I said, "what happened when you got on board?"

It did not come out readily. The pair of them were absurdly self-conscious about it, both the slick little Cockney and the huge American. They looked like a couple of guilty schoolboys.

"Out with it," I said.

"There was an officer on deck when we came up the gangway," said Collins. "First mate—at least that's what you'd think from his uniform. He looked at the three of us pretty sharp as he saw us coming along. Bit startled too. Funniest fix I've ever been in. The bloke who brought us wanted to tell the officer that he wanted our throats cut, but of course he couldn't say so in front of us. And I knew Lindy here was all set to do something, but I didn't know what it was."

"And what was it?" I asked, when I could not bear the silence any longer.

"We came together on the deck, the four of us, just below the bridge, and we sort of looked at one another, each of us waiting for the other one to speak. It was like what you see in the movies, where two cowboys are wondering who is going to reach for his gun first."

"And who did?" I asked.

The little Cockney had been voluble enough up to now, but now he was parting with his words as if they were teeth out of his head. "Nobody said nothing.

160

The officer opened his mouth, but I never knew what he was going to say, because opening his mouth just pulled Lindy's trigger. You wouldn't think he could be so quick, seeing what a great big lump he is. He took our man by the back of the neck and he took the officer by the back of his neck, and he brought them together quick as lightning. I never saw him do it. What I did see was the two of them knocked out clean. Our little fellow was out cold, and the top of his head had hit the officer's face, so you can guess what the officer looked like. Or perhaps you can't, sir. Lindy just dropped 'em on the deck, and he says, 'Come on,' to me, and he starts for the bridge like the way a greyhound comes out of the trap at dog races. We'd only just started when someone came out of the galley.

"He saw us running for the ladder and those two fellows lying on the deck, and he shouted out loud. Talking about it afterwards, I found out that what he shouted was '*Achtung!*' Which is the German for 'Look out!' In case you don't know, sir, but I didn't know it at the time—I just heard a foreigner shouting.

"So, just as we were coming on the bridge, we met the captain coming out of the chartroom with a gun in his hand.

"We were nearly face to face when we met, and Lindy hit him—only just once. Coo! The captain's feet came up off the deck and he went over backwards, and the gun went through the air over the rail and fell into the bay. There was two or more men coming out of the chartroom behind the captain, and they had guns, too, but things were still going on so quickly they didn't have a chance to use them. Lindy reached out and grabbed them both, and they all three jammed together in one tight lump in the chartroom doorway —you see how big Lindy is, sir. Then they came tumbling out on the bridge still locked together. They walked all over the captain. Coo! I wouldn't like to have Lindy walking up and down my stomach. Would you, sir?

"They were twirling round by me, and as they twirled I saw a hand sticking out with a gun in it, and of course I grabbed. Cripes! I nearly wished I hadn't; the thing went off. You know what those automatics are like, sir; the man who was holding it never thought to let go of the trigger, of course. There was bullets everywhere for a second or two. Don't know how they come to miss me. I didn't know what to do for a bit. But there were more people running up on to the bridge, and I knew I had to attract somebody's attention quick, or Lindy and me were goners. But there was the string you blow the whistle with . . . What's the nautical name of it, Lindy?"

"Lanyard," said Lindstrom patiently.

"Lanyard," said Collins; "so I went for that and I pulled it. Cripes! Have you ever been on the bridge when the whistle's gone off, sir? It all but scared me out of my clothes—nearly dropped the blessed lanyard. I went on pulling and the whistle went on bellowing, and then I left off pulling steadily and blew off a whole lot of little toots, like the alarm signal when you sight a sub. What I wanted was for the people on shore to guess there was something wrong."

"They guessed, all right," grinned Lindstrom—

"the Army and the Navy and the Coast Guard and the Customs."

"It wasn't long before they were there either. They just came pouring on board, and they had everybody prisoner in two shakes of a duck's tail. They had us prisoner too, until I explained. But after that it was all right. So you see how it was, sir."

"I don't see anything of the sort," I said. "I am still guessing. Who were these people on board the *Duncansby Head*?"

"Jerries, of course," said Collins airily, "just jerries."

"But—" I said.

Lindstrom interposed to explain. "She'd been captured by that surface raider out in the Atlantic," he said. "The first shot knocked her radio antenna down and she never had a chance to give warning. So there they had her, with papers and everything complete. All they had to do was to put explosives on board her and give her an English-speaking crew dressed up in the old uniforms. If you ask me, I guess German surface ships carry English-speaking seamen just for that purpose. She was outward-bound in ballast for Iquique for nitrate. No trouble at all to get her into the canal."

For Lindstrom, this was a remarkably long speech, and when he had finished it he drank beer as if he had said every word there was to say on the subject.

"Now look here," I said. "What were they going to do in the canal?"

"Wreck it," answered Lindstrom simply.

"Wreck it?" I repeated.

"Yes. Our Navy got a pretty good idea of what they had in mind when they went through the ship. They'd

163

got a piece of the stern cut away just over the props, so that it would fall out when they were ready, and a couple of makeshift torpedo tubes mounted inside. And they'd got explosive charges in the bottom of her, too, so that they could blow the bottom out of the ship. As far as our people could make out, they were going to wait until they were passing out of the upper lock at Gatun. Then they were going to blow the charges and sink the ship with the gate jammed open, and as they did that they were going to fire the torpedoes at the lower gate and blow that too. It would have been a couple of months before they got anything along the canal after that."

"That would have been a nasty business," I said.

"It would," agreed Collins.

A further light was dawning on me as I thought over the story that I had just heard.

"When did you tell me that this happened?"

"December sixth," said the two of them simultaneously, grinning.

"The attack on Pearl Harbor came next day. They were meant to coincide?"

"I think it goes deeper than that," said Lindstrom. "I think it was the Germans' capturing the *Duncansby Head* that set off the Pearl Harbor attack. When they captured her and realised what they could do with her, it was an extra bribe to get the Japs to come in. We had a lot of our ships in the Atlantic then, you know, sir."

"God bless my soul!" I said. I could say nothing more until I thought I could see a flaw in their story. "But why did they let that man go ashore who was wearing the gunner's uniform?"

Lindstrom wagged his head with infinite wisdom. "Our men aren't so dumb," he explained. "If a ship came into Limon Bay and nobody went ashore on the tear in Colón, we'd know something was up. They were quite right—the Germans, I mean."

"But his feet were too big," said Collins; "he couldn't wear the regulation boots. That's what gave him away, and how we happen to be here, sir."

"I still don't see how you are," I said.

"Oh, they gave us leave," said Collins; "they brought us up before the American admiral and he asked us what we'd like.

"Well, when I volunteered for this sea-going job, it was because I wanted to see New York, and I made five voyages and never got there. And Lindy here, he'd joined the Navy to see the world, but they didn't include New York in the world either. So we asked for a week's leave each and passage to New York."

"And what did he say?"

"He laughed. He gave Lindy leave like a shot. But after he had got leave for me, he told me he wouldn't do it again for anybody. Not for anyone in the British service. It took five cables to London to get the War Office to understand that an American admiral was troubling himself to get leave for an English Tommy."

"And that's not all," added Lindstrom. "He said we had to have money to spend if we had a week in New York. And after that experience he wouldn't try to get us any extra—not even from Washington, and especially not from London.

"He gave us a hundred dollars each, and that

was Secret Service money. It's Secret Service money that we're drinking now."

Lindstrom raised his beer to his lips with a massive gesture.

"I didn't think it tasted like beer," said Collins.

Well, that is what they told me. I know you should not repeat rumours. If it is true, I cannot see any reason why the American Government should not tell us about it. I know you should not repeat rumors, but I think you ought to know this.

Rendezvous

Actually this story is fiction, but it lies so close to fact that it had to be shown to the Navy censor. Certain technical details were scissored out, but the essential story remains.

Neither the Fleet oiler, at anchor in the bay, nor her warrant bosun, could be called good looking. Ships of war generally have a functional beauty, resulting from the wholehearted efforts of their designers to make them fighting vessels, and nothing other than fighting vessels, but this ship was only a self-propelled oil tank, and the guns she carried had the appearance of being stuck on as an afterthought—as indeed they were. Furthermore, she was disfigured by great cliffs of cargo on her cargo deck amidships, stacks and stacks of cardboard boxes, wooden boxes, steel boxes.

The curious eye which read the labels on those boxes would be mildly surprised to see what they contained: the candy bars which the American public were learning to do without; peanuts and canned fruit; evaporated vegetables; and along with these packages were others of deadly weapons, of clothing, of tools, seemingly higgledy-piggledy, but actually laid out on the deck in a definite scheme which had cost the supply officer a good deal of thought, and which had cost the crew much labour to execute.

The crew and the warrant bosun were at ease now, reaping the reward of a day of severe toil. A few were on watch, manning those guns and telephones which even in a protected anchorage are never left unmanned by day or night. A few were sleeping; but all the rest were gathered in the darkened mess hall.

Across the centre of the hall hung a screen, and on this screen was being projected a motion picture; half the men had to see the picture back to front, because they had to look at it from the back of the screen, but nobody minded that very much. A motion picture was a luxury from any point of view.

The warrant bosun put a fresh stick of chewing gum into his mouth and prepared to enjoy himself. He was on the right side of the screen, he had an excellent day's work behind him, and in two minutes' time he would hear Bing Crosby sing. After that would come a whole night in bed and an easy day tomorrow. All was right with the world.

Yet while the warrant bosun was unwrapping that piece of gum, a light on shore suddenly trained itself upon the ship and began to wink and flash a staccato Morse code.

A signalman upon the bridge recorded the message and slid down the ladder with it to the captain.

In the mess hall, an opened door let in a shaft of light which blotted out the motion picture, and a voice came bellowing in to drown Bing Crosby's: "Go to your station, all special sea details."

Switches clicked, and light flooded the mess hall. Bing Crosby's song came to an inglorious end.

"Hell!" said the warrant bosun, getting to his feet along with everyone else.

The bosun's mate who had brought the message caught sight of him, blinking in the light.

"Cap'n says to prepare the ship for fuelling at sea."

"Hell!" said the warrant bosun again. He pushed out through the mob in the alleyway into his cabin and switched on the light there. On the bulkhead at the foot of his bed were stuck a couple of pictures of nude women; on his desk stood a photograph of his wife. He reached for his sheepskin coat, struggled into it, plunged out of his cabin on to the cargo deck and made his way forward along the catwalk.

Darkness was closing in; the wind was cold, causing the warrant bosun to turn up the collar of his sheepskin coat as he took his post on the exposed forecastle. The light was still flashing from the shore station, and while the anchor was actually being hove in, a motor whaleboat ran alongside, and an officer, the gold cord of the staff around his shoulder, handed a final packet of orders to the captain. Clearly, something out of the ordinary was in the wind, some important strategic move, but the warrant bosun did not care about that. Strategy was something for captains to worry about, and admirals, and the staff at Washington. His own affair, now that the anchor was in and the ship was heading out into the bay, was to prepare for fuelling at sea.

There can be gunnery specialists and radio specialists, engineers and torpedomen, but they are newcomers to the sea, while the boatswain traces his descent straight back to Noah. Everything that makes a ship a ship is in his department; it is not his concern whether she is a fighting machine or not, but it is his business to make sure that she is efficient for sea. All ropework and cordage are in his province, all blocks and tackle, cables and anchors. Your skilled specialist rating may go all his life at sea without having to tie any knot except in his shoelaces, but the bosun has to be able to knot and splice, to be familiar with the foibles of Manila line, to know how to reeve a block, just as did his predecessor in the days of Paul Jones.

The warrant bosun took his station under the break of the forecastle while the pipes went squealing through the ship.

"Rig all fuelling at sea gear. Rig all fuelling at sea gear."

Men came scrambling through the darkness to take up their stations and, as they did so, the ship reached the open water outside the bay and made her first plunge into the rollers that awaited her. Her tank deck was no more than six feet above the surface, with nothing more than a wire string along stanchions for additional protection. Dense spray came splashing through the darkness, and then, with a hiss and a roar, a wave top came slapping over the tank deck, surging across from one side to the other, drenching every man at his station. Even on the catwalk overhead, the spray was sufficiently dense to wet thoroughly any man taking the short walk from the midships superstructure to the forecastle. And the first wave top was only the precursor of an infinite number of others, leaping on board with montonous regularity, sousing the men at work on the tank deck, and promising to go on sousing them with the same monotonous regularity for as long as they should stay there, eight hours or twenty-eight hours as their duty should dictate.

With the sublime impartiality of any natural force, the sea soused the warrant bosun as well as the men working under him, and the brisk breeze set up by the ship's progress through the night chilled him, too. In idle moments, he dug his hands deep into his side pockets and cursed fittingly with the same monotonous regularity as the waves came aboard and the wind blew.

But the idle moments were few, for there was an infinity of things to be done. Booms had to be rigged. Hose had to be coupled up. Seven men, working as a team, could just manhandle each length of hose into position so as to couple it to its fellows, stumbling along in the darkness over the valves and pipes which at irregular and irritating intervals interrupted the smooth expanse of the tank deck. Other teams, meanwhile, were getting out the lines from the fore-peak—the five-inch Manila ropes which lay there, stowed and tagged under the bosun's supervision, ready for just this emergency, so that in the dark they could be got out and and taken back to where they were needed, with the least confusion and delay.

It had to be in the dark; that was imperative. Not the smallest glimmer of light could be allowed to disclose the ship's position as she plunged through the night. Anywhere there might be submarines lying in ambush, awaiting just such an immensely profitable target as the Fleet oiler. At any moment, a torpedo might come hurtling against the side, to transform the ship into a pillar of flame. The warrant bosun's men must find their way about the deck, must lay their hands with certainty upon any item of their infinitely varied equipment, without the assistance even of a momentary flash from a pocket lamp.

In the dark, they had to reeve their tackle, tie their rolling hitches and their clove hitches, rig the booms, and, in the dark, the warrant bosun had to make his way around the deck, giving orders and assistance, feeling with his hands like a blind man to make sure that the work was properly done, correcting mistakes and correlating the efforts of the twenty different teams of men all labouring frantically together, whipped by the wind and soused by the sea.

The towline had to be got out and faked down on the deck ready for use as smoothly as any skein of yarn, for, if given the opportunity, it will kink and twist, so that in use it will jump off the niggerhead and take half a dozen lives and—possibly more important—delay the fuelling of the Fleet.

In his twenty years at sea, the warrant bosun had seen all kinds of mishaps, and now in the darkness he was guarding against them all, as well as against all the unexpected and unforeseen possibilities that can arise with a sea running and a wind blowing and dead-weight masses of forty thousand tons manoeuvering in close proximity. He had a willing lot of men working for him, and even the recruits among them had acquired plenty of experience during the hectic weeks of their service, but none of them had his own vast experience and enormous wisdom.

When it comes to ropes and tackle and heading

off the forces of nature, there can be no short cut as good as twenty years of work at sea. It takes that long to learn to be able to tell by touch whether a boom is properly rigged so that it can be relied upon to bear the weight of a many-ton hose in a rough sea.

After hours of pitch-darkness and rough seas, the warrant bosun could confidently report to the first lieutenant that the ship was prepared. He peered at the face of his watch—for the first time since starting work—and he felt a flow of modest pride at what he had been able to do.

"Just as well," was all the first lieutenant said. "We're starting oiling now."

A tanker is only a tanker, but a Fleet oiler is something very different. It is the existence of the Fleet oiler which has changed the whole complexion of naval strategy. She has the equipment which enables her to supply the Fleet with fuel without it becoming necessary to return to a base. Speed and equipment are essential to the Fleet oiler, but it is equally essential that she should have the men to make use of them, whose skill makes possible the delicate operation of fuelling a fleet at sea. A destroyer operating at high speed can consume the whole of her fuel in a few days. She would be helpless then without the aid of the Fleet oiler, and if the destroyer were absent, the battleship would be endangered. In the vast distances of the Pacific, it would be impossible to sweep the seas were it not for the Fleet oilers and the men who man them. It is dangerous work that they do, and there is small enough honour or glory about it in the eyes of the public.

"We're starting oiling now," said the first lieutenant.

The warrant bosun went up to the spray-swept forecastle. It was still too dark for anything to be seen, on either side, but right ahead, by straining his eyes, he could just make out the tiniest glimmer of a light; ahead of them, a battleship was showing that light directly astern, shaded so that any prowling Japanese submarine could take no advantage of it. It is hard for a submarine to stalk her prey from anywhere except forward of the beam.

The light grew gradually closer, and the warrant bosun knew that on the bridge the captain was steering the Fleet oiler so as to pass as close to the light as possible. Then the light disappeared from the warrant bosun's gaze, as the nearing of the two ships took him out of the beam. Peering through the spray and balancing himself on the plunging forecastle, he could at last make out the huge bulk of the battleship, an immense deep shadow in the surrounding dark. A dead weight of forty thousand tons, driving through the sea as fast as any whale, it was bound to set up fantastic eddies and suction currents all round it.

The warrant bosun knew enough about those conditions to appreciate the skill and nerve of the Fleet oiler's captain, who was having to steer his ship through those eddies close enough to the battleship for a line to be thrown across the gap, and yet not so close as to touch. Forty thousand tons dead weight, heaving and plunging in a rough sea, will deal a blow that would crush in the side of a stouter vessel than a floating oil tank.

Slowly the Fleet oiler overtook the huge black

shadow. Bow overlapped stern, and the warrant bosun could now see the battleship in vague profile, the immense turrets and the colossal guns, the staggered upper works, and then the unmistakable profile of the bow. The two ships were in such close proximity to each other that the sound of the waves leaping and crashing in the narrow space between them was clearly audible over the wind.

"Let's have it!" said the warrant bosun to the shadowy men at his side; and he did not say "it"; he substituted a dirty noun for the pronoun, as unnecessarily as ever. He took the heaving line in his hands, deftly seized half a dozen coils in his right hand while his left loosely held the remainder, and whirled the weight with the full strength of his arm. The weight soared off into the darkness, and the line ran smoothly out from his left hand.

Had it been daylight, the warrant bosun would have fired a line out of a gun, but in darkness that would mean a revealing flash. Human muscle and skill had to take the place of a gun, and if the line were badly thrown, if it fell short and had to be recoiled and re-thrown, five minutes would be wasted, and, with many ships to fuel, a similar mistake at each would make a total of many minutes lost, and in so many minutes . . .

The warrant bosun did not know that Nelson had once said that at sea five minutes can make the difference between victory and defeat, but he felt that truth in his bones after twenty years in the Navy.

The weight shot off into the darkness, trailing the line behind it, and the warrant bosun uttered a grunt of morose satisfaction at feeling the line catch and hold. Someone on the battleship's forecastle had seized it. Megaphones shouted orders over the wind, and the heaving line ran steadily out to the battleship. There was a two-inch messenger line attached to the heaving line—the warrant bosun was responsible for the vital knot which joined them—and, by the time the two-inch line was being hauled into the battleship, the warrant bosun was ready to follow it with a 3½-inch line, and that was followed by a five-inch line, and that was strong enough to have entrusted to it the immense Manila towline on which the rest of the operation depended.

From other parts of the ship, other heaving lines had been thrown, other messengers passed, now that the two ships were riding together more or less comfortably harnessed together with the heavy Manila. The warrant bosun stood by the niggerhead, as the ships surged and plunged over the waves. It was up to him to ease the strain or take it up, keeping the ships at a constant distance apart without allowing the towline to break under the continual jerks to which the waves subjected it. If that line should part, everything else, including the precious hoses which the booms were beginning to swing out over the gap, would be torn asunder.

On the bridges, the captains were fighting with screw and rudder against the other tendency of the ships to crash together, although the possible damage from that could be minimised now by the nests of fenders—clusters of three fenders together, each cluster weighting a quarter of a ton—which the warrant bosun had hung over the side at strategic points.

The warrant bosun left his place beside the towline long enough to hurry aft and supervise the swinging out of the booms which were pushing the hoses out toward the battleship. It was only a matter of faith that they were doing that; it was too dark to see them. A loftier wave than usual squeezed into the narrow passage between the ships, came slapping over the deck and soused the warrant bosun even more thoroughly than before, and he said the same words over again; it was not a very extensive vocabulary that he had. But with the booms functioning properly, he still had other matters to attend to. It was not merely oil which the battleship needed; the Fleet oiler was a sort of fairy godmother to the whole task force, which had only to express a Cinderella wish to find it instantly granted.

One of the first things the messenger lines had taken over to the battleship had been a telephone, and now eager officers in the battleship were pouring out their desires and their needs into the sympathetic ear of the supply officer. Mail, of course, was the most important thing in everyone's mind, and the Fleet oiler carried two weeks' mail for the two thousand men in the battleship—thirty thousand letters or so at a conservative estimate. The sacks of mail were all conveniently handy for transfer, but when it came to the other supplies demanded, it was a test of the foresight of the supply officer.

Fresh food, the battleship wanted; bread; cylinders of oxygen for the battleship's plane pilots; peanuts and candy; drums of lubricating oil; and all these miscellaneous stores had to be transferred to the battleship across an open space of tossing sea, and that was the warrant bosun's job. He had to supervise the whips secured to the king post. Two aerial ropeways were stretched across to the battleship, and running on each rope was a block, and suspended from the blocks were immense buckets of stout canvas.

From each bucket ran two ropes, one to the battleship and one to the oiler, and by pulling on one or the other, the bucket and its contents could be sent back and forth across the water. The men had to work fast, with the water swirling round their knees.

All those stores must be transferred by the time the battleship was fuelled. Five minutes might make the difference between victory and defeat, and already the quick-release valves had been clamped down upon the battleship's flanges, and the pumps were filling the thirsty tanks.

The warrant bosun saw to it that his whips were properly rigged, manned and working, and then he hurried forward again to have another look at that precious Manila towline. Everything was all right there. An ignorant person might expect a breathing space for the warrant bosun now, but he would have to be a very ignorant person.

"When the hell is daylight coming?" said the warrant bosun to himself. For the first time, he had taken a false step and fallen headlong over a valve on the deck, the presence of which he had momentarily forgotten. He swore at the valve and he swore at himself, at the darkness of the night and at the roughness of the sea, as he plunged on round the decks like a squirrel in a cage. With every man and every rope in the ship hard at work, his attention was needed at all points at once.

Daylight was at hand, however. The sky to the east was growing pale, and the ships wallowing along, like drunken men hand in hand, were becoming more and more visible—the massive, solid beauty of the battleship and the grim, harsh ugliness of the Fleet oiler. Faces could be made out in one ship from the next, and friends could recognise one another. The task force had spent not days, but weeks at sea, ploughing monotonously through the grey water in unceasing watch, and this brief interval spent alongside a new arrival was a blessed respite, a cupful of the water of variety in the thirsty desert of hateful monotony. On the battleship, there were men with leisure to enjoy it, men with time to stop and grin and wave their arms, but in the Fleet oiler every man was busy, and their recent life had not been monotonous.

The growing daylight revealed more and more of the task force, so that an observer could form some notion of the elaborate staff work needed for fuelling at sea. It was a fighting formation, as it had to be, even while at the same time it was performing a peaceful evolution, and those precious minutes had to be saved. The moment one ship had completed her fuelling, another had to be ready to take her place, leaving her fighting station in ample time while another ship filled the gap in the screen.

The warrant bosun hurried across to look after the business of casting off, and the battleship drew slowly ahead under the impulse of the quickened beat of her propellers, her crew waving farewell. An aircraft carrier was awaiting attention, but the warrant bosun might at least have spared time for a friendly wave of the arm if his eye had not caught sight of the searchlight winking at the flagship's signal bridge. "Expedite," said those dots and dashes. The warrant bosun spelled them out for himself.

"Expedite!" said the warrant bosun. "Expedite . . ." He went on to say all the things he had said before, in practically the same order, dirt and blasphemy intermixed. Expedite, indeed!

The warrant bosun had not sat down since Bing Crosby's song had been interrupted yesterday, and he saw no possibility of sitting down until tomorrow. He was wet and hungry and weary but the Fleet oiler was moving up alongside the carrier, and the warrant bosun had to leave off swearing. Those messenger lines had to be passed, and he could save five minutes if he made quite sure that they went over at the first attempt.

Minutes are always of importance in war, and today they were of more importance than ever, although the warrant bosun did not know it. Away over the horizon were two factors that the warrant bosun knew nothing of: There was a storm approaching, and there was a Japanese force steaming across the task force's front.

To intercept and destroy that convoy, the task force must steam fast and far, and must be fully fuelled. If that storm were to arrive in time to interrupt the fuelling, the Japs would escape, and not merely escape, but would land their reinforcements on one of those dots on the map, the strategic importance of which has only become clear to us since 1941. Ultimate victory, the final triumph of the United Nations, perhaps did not hinge on destroying that convoy, but much depended on it, all the same: the lives of many Americans, the possible duration of the war, and, along with that, the future of American citizens yet unborn. It was enough to justify the admiral's impatience when he hoisted the signal which made the warrant bosun swear.

The aircraft carrier needed gasoline as well as fuel oil, and as the boom swung the hose across the gap, the bosun's mates hurried through the Fleet oiler, shrilling on their pipes.

"The smoking lamp is out throughout the ship," they called, which is the way the Navy says "No smoking". The warrant bosun said his words over again, every one of them. He had not had time even to light a cigarette, and the order annoyed him just as much as did the admiral's "Expedite."

There were a couple of sick men to transfer, ratings with broken bones who were in need of the comfort of the Fleet oiler's big sick bay, the diagnosis possible with the Fleet oiler's X-ray apparatus, and the ultimate transfer to a hospital. The warrant bosun made it his special business to supervise the work—helpless men strapped into immobility on their wire stretchers but stolidly fatalistic during their dizzy passage along the rope. The sea was working up with the approaching storm; it needed nice judgement to get the men down on the deck without a jar, and the warrant bosun only had just time to hand them over to the doctor before running forward again over the swirling decks to look after his towlines.

Battleships and destroyers and cruisers; one by one they came up alongside the Fleet oiler and drank thirstily from her hoses, like little pigs coming up to the mother sow, all through the long, weary day of wet and cold and increasing fatigue. It was twelve hours of hard work, but what the warrant bosun did not fully appreciate was the fact that it was also twelve hours of advance toward the enemy, twelve hours of movement to intercept that Japanese convoy. The ability to fuel at sea in any weather short of a gale extended the radius of action of the task force by hundreds—thousands—of miles, and that ability turned on how well the warrant bosun had kept his cordage in condition, how well he had maintained his gear and how well he handled it when the time came.

It was the Fleet oiler and her warrant bosun that made victory possible. Those enormous battleships over there, imposing with their turrets and fire-control towers, were no whit more important than this homely oil tanker.

It might even be expressed more forcibly still: The admiral at the battleship's bridge, the admiral with the broad gold on his sleeve, irascibly signalling "Expedite," was at that particular moment a less important person than the warrant bosun, wet through, worn out, and yet still swinging out the boom and hose with all the accurate judgement of twenty years of experience.

The work had begun before daylight; and night was about to fall when the last line was cast off and faked down. The warrant bosun had intercepted the "Expedite" signal, but chance did not bring to his attention the "Well done" signal which the admiral sent over—the highest compliment which it was in the admiral's power to pay.

The warrant bosun was too busy getting his gear secured, ready for the storm which was upon them. It did just pass through his mind that they had finished in the nick of time, that if the heaving lines had not been properly thrown, if a single line had parted at any time during the day, if an hour had been lost, whether in one single catastrophe or in dribs and drabs through the day, they would never have completed the fuelling before the storm, but he did not know enough about the strategical situation to make any further deduction.

All he knew was that he was wet and tired, and the gear had to be secured, lines made up and stowed, and the axes put away, which all day long had lain ready on the deck to cut the ships free in the event of an attack. The Fleet had vanished into the unknown darkness, and the oiler was then heading for the bay again.

He finished his work; the gale was upon them now, the sea breaking green over the tank deck, and even over the catwalk, while the ship, her tanks empty, rolled fantastically over the heavy sea. The warrant bosun clawed his way aft through the roaring wet dark, guided by experience to the door into the after superstructure. He heaved himself over the coaming, and down the alleyway with its faint red light. He switched on the light in his cabin and stood there, the water streaming from his clothes on the steel deck. The light shone on the photograph of his wife and the two nude pictures. It was twenty-eight hours since he had last laid his eyes on them.

"Hell!" said the warrant bosun to himself; that was the only word of the many which he said to himself which can be reproduced.

He began to peel off his wet clothes. This was a month with thirty-one days in it, so that his pay for a day amounted to ten dollars and six cents, with another dollar fifty-one for the extra four hours. So that, from the time of leaving his cabin to the time of re-entering it, he had earned $11.57, and, during that time, he had perhaps shortened by a couple of months a war costing ten million a day.